T0194313

A
Murder
In Time

GARY T. BRIDEAU

iUniverse®

A MURDER IN TIME

iUniverse books may be ordered through booksellers or by contacting:

iUniverse
1663 Liberty Drive
Bloomington, IN 47403
www.iuniverse.com
1-800-Authors (1-800-288-4677)

ISBN: 978-1-6632-0372-4 (sc)
ISBN: 978-1-6632-0373-1 (e)

Print information available on the last page.

iUniverse rev. date: 06/19/2020

Character Descriptions

George Bentwood: a clean-cut man in his 40s, clad in black dress pants and a dark blue shirt, moved to a small town south of Knoxville, Tennessee. Saw a three-acre farm with its white picket fence for sale and bought it. George invented the Time Arch and married Cynthia.

Cynthia Celestina Atwater: a tall slender woman in her late 30s with long wavy brown hair. She is a modest woman in every sense of the word and has never fooled around with a man. She loves the Lord and married George.

Ruth White: a tall single slender woman in her late 30s that looked like a skeleton with skin pulled over it, with short black hair. She is devious, sly, and cunning, and knows how to dominate men by using her feminine wiles.

Art Boulder: an inventor who is an easy-going man in his mid-30s who is short with light brown hair, likes to wear old ragged shirt and pants. Dates Ruth but has the hots for Cynthia.

Pastor Mark Tumwater a tall godly man in his 20s with neatly combed brown hair, wire-rimmed glasses. Wears black pants and white shirts. He is easygoing, compassionate, and understanding and will go the extra mile for someone without question.

Pastor Larry Farnsworth: a single short man in his 40s who likes to wear torn jeans and t-shirts and has a vegetable garden. This pastor is devious and tricked Ruthie into going all the way with him one evening at his house and uses her for his selfish means.

Ruthie Susan White: a tall thin single woman in her 30s with blond hair done up in a ponytail likes to wear jeans and t-shirts. Ruthie's parents taught her that no matter what happens she had to do what she was told and not complain about it. When she dated a young pastor, Mister

Farnsworth, who is an authoritative type of person and got in bed with him. From then on, her morals went downhill and she became cunning and sly just like Mister Farnsworth and let him take from her whatever he desires.

Don Hollister: a man in his mid-40s with short gray hair wears coveralls and has the hots for Cynthia and will not believe that she is married to George. Don is pushy, and bossy and expects Cynthia to do what he says. He tries to get Cynthia to notice him by doing things that will get her attention. Cynthia thinks Don is nauseating.

Rubin Walt: is a tall husky man in his mid-30s with broad shoulders. He is crude, rude, and rough and always manhandles Cynthia every time he visits her cottage.

Martha Dirtbottom: A woman who is 5 foot 2, in her mid-20s with shoulder-length dark, brown wavy hair. She is a Christian and is best buds with Ruthie.

Rosella Puckett: is a petite 33-year-old woman who is 5'3" feet tall, with brown hair. Is Dating Thoralf Greystone,

Thoralf Greystone: is in his 30s, has difficulty hearing, blind in one eye and has trouble walking because of a balance problem. He had brain cancer, hydrocephalus, hemiparesis, kidney failure, liver problems, and melanoma and is in a wheelchair. His real name is Thoralf Oakley Bjornstad but goes by **Thoralf Greystone**

Callie Swanson: A single 31-year-old woman 5' 5" tall with short wavy black hair. Is a writer and a few cents short of a dollar. And is dating a man named Bo Sidewinder.

Bo Sidewinder; is Callie's age with short brown hair and likes to jog.

Patrick O'Brien: Is a leprechaun doctor and is married to Alexis Nimswicky.

Alexis Rosenthal Nimswicky: is a petite 4'7" woman who is 30 years old, has bright red hair done up in a pixie and is a jokester.

Sylvia: a 30-year-old woman who is 5 foot 9 dressed in black with short brown hair married to Bruce Birdson.

Bruce Jay Birdson: is 30 years old with dark brown hair done up in a ponytail and a mustache and owned a ranch in Wickenburg, Arizona.

Breana Chase: a 5' 8" tall, 37-year-old woman with medium length brown hair. Is married to. Ray Coffey.

Ray Coffey: A tall gentleman in his late 20s with short light brown hair likes to wear dark gray suit and tie and is in law enforcement.

Asami: A short Japanese woman in her late 20s, 5 foot 6 is married to Harry Grubs.

Harry Grubs: a 35-year-old man, 5 foot 9 inches tall with short blonde hair with a van dike. Is the ranch security on Bruce's ranch. But also lives and works in the Hassayampa River Preserve A short distance from Bruce's ranch.

Mosey: is a single 5 ft 5-inch tall oriental woman in her early twenties with a black belt in karate.

Connie, a five foot five, twenty-five-year-old woman, with an attractive perky figure, short brown hair. Her hazel eyes sparkle when she talks. Is married to Dan Comings

Dan Comings: Is a typical nerd who is six feet tall, cleanly shaven and had his own lab.

Beebe Tomson: A young petite woman in her early 30s wears gold wire-rimmed glasses. with dark brown hair done up in a pixie. Likes to wear jeans and a white t-shirt.

Maybell Fits Art Boulders girlfriend she is a cute 5-foot five blonde hair with a great figure. She lives on 400 Fairway Lane in Abingdon, Virginia and Art sees her every so often. Lived in 1885 and died in 1954,

Storyline

George Bentwood moved to Tennessee from Massachusetts and bought a farm. Because he is gifted in electronics he invents something called the Time Arch. So, he could travel back in time, bye specific items to sell them as antiques in his time. George saves a woman named Cynthia and marries her. Only to find out that all the evidence says that she's a psychotic killer. But there is something about Cynthia that says that she is innocent. After they hire a woman named Ruthie to help them solve the murder. Ruthie tries to use her sexuality to seduce George so she could have the Time Arch for her own research. But becomes romantically involved with some of the men of the past.

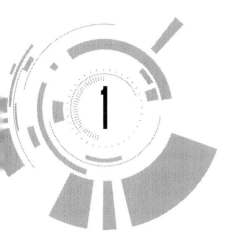

1

Exposed

George Bentwood, a clean-cut man in his forties, clad in black dress pants and a dark blue shirt, moved to a small town south of Knoxville, Tennessee. He drove up route 332 and saw a three-acre farm with its white picket fence broken down for sale. He stared at the shopping plaza on the right and a housing complex on the other two sides, took the sign, went to the Realtor, and said, "I want to buy that farm on route 332."

The Realtor stared at George and said, "I hope you are not planning to farm it because it would make a great place for a water park."

"I plan to live there and turn the barn into a museum about the town."

"Yeah right."

"Are you going to sell me the farm or not?"

"Okay mister It is your money."

After George bought the farm, the first thing he did was to repair the picket fence, had the house painted white, decorated the inside to resemble the mid-1890s. He then restored the red barn and had electrical equipment delivered there.

In a room in the loft ten feet by ten, George constructed an arch 8 feet tall and five feet wide made out of die-cast Aluminum eight inches thick against the far wall. He then wrapped the arch with two magnetic coils with opposite polarities and encased them with his invention called the HJO Capacitor which powers the magnetic field around the Time Arch, interrupting the delicate balance between the past and future, allowing him to easily slip through time.

George then dressed in the dark gray tweed suit and a silk top hat. Looked at himself in the mirror and said, "Ready or not 1890 here I come." He activated the Time Arch then vanished in the blue glow of the arch and found himself in the same barn in early May of 1890. A short Well-dressed man entered the barn with a young couple saying, "This spread will make a perfect place for you and your little ones."

George held up a bag of gold saying, "I'll give you half of this bag of gold for the house, barn and the fifteen acres of land."

"You have yourself a farm, Mister!"

The young man held his wife's hand and complained, "Hey. You told my wife and me that we could have the farm, now you're selling it to him."

The Realtor stated, "I forgot to tell you that it goes to the highest bidder and can you beat his bid?"

The young couple hung their heads and turned to leave. George shouted, "Lady! Would you like to sell your pretty red parasol?" then showed her a hand full of gold nuggets.

The woman looked at her fancy parasol, then stared at the gold nuggets in George's hand, quickly gave him the parasol, grabbed the gold, and left with her husband.

The Realtor stared at George in wonderment and question, "What are you going to do with a ladies parasol?"

George smiled and said, "I collect them."

The Realtor stared at George and said Mr. you are one strange man. In joy your farm, I will see you later."

Back in his normal time, George sold the ladies One of a kind Parasols to an antique dealer in the next town for $1500.00.

Later, George stood in front of the barn, slowly studied his 15-acre farm, and wondered how he could put all that land to good use. When the thought hit him, how much damage did he do to the community by changing the timeline? He then muttered, "That shopping mall and that housing community shouldn't make a difference to the town's growth. But I know the town isn't as prosperous as it used to be."

Just them a twelve-year-old boy clad in jeans and a t-shirt raced in on his bicycle, handed George a flyer and sped off. He stared at it and wondered, "What do they mean fix the dam before it is too late? I just read in the town paper yesterday that the town's people were praising Mayor Thomas for renovating the dam two years ago."

George quickly drove to the dam and was appalled at its deplorable condition. Saw a fisherman casting his line in the river and inquired, "I thought Mayor Thomas fixed the dam. What did he spend all that tax money on?"

The man stared at George, laughed, and asked, "What have you been smoking buddy? The Mayor is Peter Gregory." The man thought for a minute then said, "Wait a minute, a Bill Thomas ran for Mayor in the last election and lost. Now if you will excuse me, buddy, I have a fish to catch."

George snapped back, "Bill Thomas had some great ideas and the backing of the large food chain store in town."

The man stared at George for three minutes before saying, "I think you have your towns mixed up because there is no food store in town because we are too small. Now, get out of here before your constant chattering scares the fish away."

Driving back to his farm George muttered, "That's right. A lot of high mucky-mucks that supported Bill Thomas for mayor and swung the election in his favor. Oh yeah, that's right. They all lived in the housing project that used to be part of the northeast part of my farm before I changed the timeline. I can't undo buying the farm and I do not want to go back in time and argue with myself about not doing that blunder. Maybe if I get married. A wife would help me think straight, but she can't be from this timeline. I could date a woman from 1890 but then how many lives would I destroy by doing that?"

George stopped in 'Gabby's Burger Joint,' saw a woman in her thirties with red hair clad in a pale blue dress enjoying a giant burger and fries, asked, "Excuse me, ma'am. If you traveled in the past and wanted to marry how would you go about doing it?"

The lady smiled and replied, "I would do a study on who was killed, save him then make him my hubby, and no I do not want to go out with you, Sir. Not because that was the worst pick-up line I have ever heard but because my boyfriend Butch would flatten you."

"I wasn't trying to get a date with you."

"You have got some nerve telling me that I am ugly."

"You are not ugly, ma'am matter of fact you are gorgeous and have a great figure."

The woman picked up her purse, hit George across the face with it shouting, "Pervert!" and stormed off.

George glanced at the lady manager staring at him. He held the side of his face and left.

For the next three and a half weeks, George searched the town records and all the murder cases but came up with nothing. As he was about to give up, an old newspaper clipping of a murdered woman fell to the floor. He picked it up and read, August 10, 1890. A 31 year old woman, Cynthia Celestina Atwater was brutally murdered while walking home from church on Sunday afternoon. If anyone knows about the killing contact the police immediately.

George showed the newspaper clipping to a police officer and asked, "Do you have any information on this woman?"

The officer glanced at the clipping and commented, "Oh yeah. The Atwater case. The killer did a number on her. Had to have a closed casket because she was so badly cut up."

"Where was Miss Atwater murdered?"

"There used to be a hauling road that ran from the old white Pentecostal church to the highway. Part of it is still there. Why are you interested in the Atwater case? Plan to solve it?"

"Yup sure do."

"Good luck Buddy."

Back at his barn, George dressed in his 1890 clothes, held his Winchester rifle in his hand. Gazed at the glowing light blue arch called The Time Arch and entered. He found the church, then hid in the woods until the service was over.

At 1:38 PM a tall slender woman in her early thirties clad in a beautiful blue checkered dress, small hat left the church, and headed for the old hauling road that went through the woods. Halfway through, a scruffy man with a beard and mustache, dressed in ragged clothes, with a crazed look in his eyes. Jumped out of the woods holding a hunting knife and knocked Miss Atwater down and was about to knife her. George fired a shot in the air and shouted, "Leave her alone!"

The man sprang to his feet and charged George. He shot the knife out of his hand, pointed the gun at his head saying, "One more step and I'll ventilate you!"

The man jumped up, knocked George down and escaped in the woods.

George helped Miss Atwater to her feet and asked, "Are you alright?"

"I tore my dress a bit but otherwise I am okay." She stared at George for a few seconds, then fell into his arms sobbing, "That man would have killed me if you didn't happen by."

"Would you like to come to my place for a cup of hot herbal tea to settle your nerves? Then I can walk you home."

"Oh, okay."

At George's place, Cynthia studied his pristine home and said, "Let me make you some good old Tennessee fried Pickles and Fried Sweet Potatoes and a pot of tea then I want to talk to you."

"Fried Pickles? You have got to be kidding me."

"You haven't lived until you have tasted my fried Pickles."

"Okay, I'm game."

A short time later, Cynthia sat a heaping plate of fried pickles along with a pot of tea on the dining room table. Poured George and herself a cup, gazed at him and said, "I want to get to know you better. But there is something about you that is off somehow, but I can't put my finger on it. You look and dress great but there is something about you that is out of place. It is if you are from another timeline or something."

"Are you into science?"

"I have studied the possibility of time travel but to do that would be impossible."

George grew nervous as he asked, "Would you like me to show you my farm?"

"And exactly what do you mean by that?" question a skeptical Cynthia.

"Nothing. I just want to show you where I live."

"And how many other women have you showed them your farm, or should I say your bedroom."

"Please forgive me. That is not what I meant. I thought a nice walk in a meadow would help you relax from your harrowing ordeal."

While they were walking through the northeast pasture, Cynthia stated, "The town is planning to build a dam across the river. But the contractor they want to use will cut corners. Which will be disastrous for the town in the future."

George picked some wildflowers, gave them to Cynthia and asked, "Is there any way someone can alert the proper authorities so he can be replaced?"

Cynthia took the flowers, smiled, and said, "Yes, I will marry you."

"But that's not what I was trying to say. Oh heck. When do you want to set the date?"

Cynthia smiles sweetly, took hold of George's left arm, pulled up his sleeve, exposed his fancy digital watch and asked, "Don't you mean in what timeline?"

"I ah, don't know what you are talking about. That watch is something new they just came out with."

"Sure, and it snows in the middle of summer. Who are you? Or should I ask when are you? Let me put that question aside for a moment and ask you how did you know I was going to be attacked on that hauling road? Don't tell me that you were hunting because there are 'No Hunting' signs all along that road and your Winchester rifle is unlike any that I have ever seen. How far in the future are you from? One hundred, two hundred years in the future? When?"

George smiled sheepishly and replied, "Let's go someplace where we can talk?"

George took Cynthia to the hayloft in the barn, she stared at him, slapped his face saying, "I am not that type of girl!"

George walked to a wall of hay, took hold of it, and pulled open a door to a room where the Time Arch was kept. He smiled and said, "This way to the year 2020."

Cynthia let out a sharp loud squeal, then shouted, "I knew it, I knew it, I knew it! Is there space travel in your time? Are there funny green aliens walking around? Tell me, tell me, tell me!"

George closed the door to the room, took Miss Atwater's hand and walked through the Time Arch.

2

Guilty or not

Cynthia Atwater walked out of the barn with George in his timeline, looked around, and inquired, "Are you joshing me about you being from the future?"

"No. Why?"

"Things look just like it does in my time. Where are the flying machines and the skyscrapers?"

George brought Cynthia into the house and asked her to pick up her beaded handbag that she left on the end table in the living room. When she did, it crumpled in her hands. She stared at George and asked in shock, "What happened to it?"

"Your handbag is over 100 years old. Come, let me show you the entertainment center in the basement."

In the basement, with indirect lighting, a shocked Cynthia gazed at a 96-inch flat-screen TV on the wall, with surround sounds, and a plush leather sofa. She flopped on the couch and said, "This is more like it."

"Would you like to go for a drive and see the sights?"

"Sure wood. Lead the way."

Cynthia stared at George's red 2018 Ford Fusion when he opened the passenger door for her. Handed her a stainless steel mug of coffee, then drove around for hours. Then stopped at a Walmart to buy her some clothes so she didn't look out of place.

When George brought her into town and showed Cynthia the 1890 curio shop, She rushed in only to find that none of the items were from her period of time. Cynthia caught the attention of the woman who owned the shop and growled, "You are a fraud and a cheat."

"What do you mean?" Question the shocked woman.

"I am an expert on 1890 curios and nothing you have is from that time period. They are cheap copies."

The owner of the shop screamed, "How dear you come to my shop and insult me like that! Get out before I throw you out!"

Cynthia picked up an item, turned it over and pointed to a small oval labile that said made in China. The shop owner smiled sheepishly and asked, "Could you get me real curios from 1890?"

"I sure could, but I get 25% from the sails."

"Deal," stated the woman, shook Cynthia's hand and said, "My name is Frances, and when can you get me those items?"

"Oh, about a week."

Back at George's farm, Cynthia made a pot of hot herbal tea, Fried Pickles, served George in the dining room. Placed a Bible on the table and asked, "Why is there an inch of dust on the Bible?"

"I never read it."

"If you expect me to marry you then you better start. Because I will not be unequally yoked to an unbeliever."

"What does reading a book have to do with us?" replied a puzzled George.

"It is the Word of God and in it, you will find all the answers, starting with eternal life."

"I always thought that if I was good enough I would make it to heaven."

"What are you going to do about your sinful nature? Because all have sinned and come short of the glory of God."

"Then what do I do?"

"Acknowledge self as Sinner, Believe that Christ rose from the dead, Confess your sins to Him, and receive Christ in your heart as your Lord and Saviour. For when Christ died on the Cross, He provided salvation, healing, deliverance, you name it Christ provided it through the Cross and Christ will put His love in your heart and will give you joy unspeakable."

"Okay, I'll go for it. Tell me how to pray."

Once George surrendered his life to Christ, Cynthia suggested, "The Time Arch should be moved to the room underneath the barn just encase the barn falls during a windstorm or somebody stumbles on The Time Room in the hayloft."

"The only thing underneath the barn is dirt, so what are you talking about?"

"Come with me and I'll show you."

In the barn, Cynthia took a broom handle, shoved it in a hole in the floor causing an eight-foot square section of the floor to spring open revealing a metal circular staircase that went down into the darkness. Next to the barn door, Cynthia pushed an old picture of a horse to one side and flipped the light switch, turning on the lights below, saying, "Don't let the grass grow under your feet George, let's go."

At the bottom of the stairs, Cynthia took hold of the broom handle and pulled it out of the slot closing the hatch.

George inquired, "Before we go any further you wanna tell me how you know about this secret cellar underneath the barn?"

Art Boulder used to own this farm and loved all kinds of contraptions and brought me down here to show me something. But I didn't trust him and hesitated to go down the winding staircase." Cynthia pointed to an old door behind the stairs saying, "That door opens to a tunnel that leads to the house."

"If you didn't come down here how did you know to take the broom handle out of the slot to close the hatch and where that door leads to?"

A frustrated Cynthia stated, "Alright, Art and I were in a serious courtship and he brought me down here to do some kissing. I did not like the idea of being down here alone with him, slapped him in his face, and went back upstairs and never saw him again."

George pointed to another door on the opposite side of the staircase and questioned, "Where does that door lead too?"

"That's Art's lab and workshop."

The rusty hinges on the door creaked as George slowly pushed it open and he stared down at the skeletal remains of a man lying on the floor with a knife in its chest. He then stated, "I take it that's Art Boulder." George gazed at Cynthia and questioned, "If this lab and workshop were only known to you and George. Who killed him?" George picked up a piece of calico clutched in the Bony right hand and stated, "This material looks like it belongs to a woman's dress since you're the only woman that knew about Art's lab, did you kill him?"

Cynthia remains silent as George studied a dark, wooden dusty oblong table cluttered with all kinds of gadgets and tools in the middle of the large room. Then in the far corner, George spotted a cot next to a small black table with a pair of fancy long black stockings stuffed in a pair of women's shoes. George then picked up a picture of Cynthia wearing the dress that matched the piece of cloth he held in his hands. He sat on the cot and asked, "You want to start from the beginning and tell me exactly what happened here? All the evidence leads to the fact that you killed Art. Why?"

A nervous Cynthia stated, "I've never been in here. and no, I didn't kill him in the heat of passion. Those are not my shoes and stockings and I own a dress with that pattern on it but I didn't kill him, you have to believe me."

"I believe you, but I'm gonna have to contact the police because I found a dead body on my property."

"If you contact the police then everybody and his brother is going to know about the secret room and your Time Arch underneath your barn."

"Good point."

A tearful Cynthia stated, "I can only think of one thing, hold me."

After George held Cynthia In his arms for ten minutes, she knelt, pulled the bone-handled hunting knife out of the skeleton, examined it, and stated, "This doesn't belong to Art, he detests hunting, and I don't own any kind of hunting knife. Hey, can I see the shoes again,"

George handed Cynthia the shoes and asked, "What's up?"

"As I said, these shoes are not mine. They look like mine but see that little Nick in the heel on the left shoe, my friend Ruth had a pair of shoes with a Nick just like that."

"Do you think Art with cheating on you?"

"I never got into it with Art so he wasn't cheating on me, but he was cautious about who he brought down here."

"Is that Art's skeletal remains or did he kill someone that snuck into his lab, panic, and left?"

Cynthia examined the green plaid suit on the skeleton, checked the white shirt and shoes then stated, "This is Art all right. At least it's his clothes."

"Do you know if Art had any broken bones?"

"Come to think of it, he broke his left leg in two places."

George took the bones out of the left pant leg and said, "This is George alright the left tibia on the leg is broken in two places." George put the leg bone on the table and questioned, "If you were never in here why is their evidence that you were!"

George picked up the picture of Cynthia, held one of the shoes she was wearing next to it, and said. "These are the same shoes you're wearing in this picture. In the picture, the top button on your left shoe is missing," George then picked up the left shoe, pointed to the missing button on the shoe and asked, "Care to explain?"

Trying to remain calm Cynthia stated, "I tell you I was never in this room. Art brought me down the stairs and wanted to bring me into his lab but I refused, slapped him in his face, and left. And that is the truth."

George put the picture and shoes down and stated, "I think I know what happened. Art brought you down here to make out. You sat on the cot and took off your shoes and your long black stockings. Art said something about your friend Ruth. You thought he was cheating on you, grab the knife on the end table, and stabbed him in a fit of rage. You then ran out the door in your bare feet, lock the door, and the hatch knowing that no one would know that Art was down here. You then bought another pair of shoes just like the ones you left in Art's workshop."

Cynthia cleared a spot on the table in the middle of the room, sat on it, and explained, "I have avoided telling you what happened because it bothers me what Art wanted me to do with him. It was a wonderful day in June of 1885, I put on my pretty blue dress with matching hat, picked up my blue, and white parasol and went for a walk. I passed an old man and his dog and a couple of kids flying kites. Then a gust of wind took my parasol out of my hand and sent it flying across a green meadow. A well-dressed, tall man with red hair and beard stop his buggy, took chase. He retrieved it and handed it back to me 5 minutes later. He introduced himself as Art Boulder and told me where we could go for a cup of coffee. As we sat at the sidewalk cafe in Knoxville, he told me jokes and funny stories that had me laughing till my side split. He then asked me if he could see me again, I smiled and said yes. He helped me back in his horse and buggy and we took a long romantic drive back home.

I was caught up in a wonderful courtship with a man and the months seemed to take wings and fly. One day in mid-September of that year, I slipped on my long black stockings that had a vertical wavy pattern on them, put on a dress that had a red and white checkered pattern. Then I walked to Art's farm several miles away. He made a fabulous meal of soup and as the clock struck noon we were eating outside at a table that was fit for a Queen. During the meal, Art kept me laughing with his witty stories. His eyes suddenly widened with eagerness and told me that he wanted to show me something in the barn. I was excited and my mind was filled with all kinds of ideas trying to figure out what it was.

In the barn, Art closed the doors, shoved a broomstick handle in a hole in the floor then turn on the lights that lit up a circular stairs and a room underneath the barn.

Underneath the barn, I stared at a door wondering what was on the other side. He opened it and explain to me all the gadgets that were in his workshop. Art than handed me a package and told me to open it. I eagerly sat on the bunk, unbuttoned my black shoes, took them off, open the package, and found a pair of black stockings with butterflies embroidered on them. I was so excited about the pretty stockings that I forgot that I was in the presence of a man. Hiked my dress up to my knees and was about to pull off my thigh-highs when the thought hit me, *"What are you doing?"* I quickly pulled my dress down to my ankles and looked up at Art standing in front of me in his string tied underwear that went down to his knees, smiling. I was so shocked that he would do something like that In my presence that all I could think of was getting away from him. So, I sprang to my feet, turned around, and ask him to get dressed. Because my mother and father taught me to be a lady and that one should not be alone in a room when a man is partially unclothed. Art stood behind me, took off his underwear, slipped his arms around my waist, and began to kiss my neck. I screamed in terror. "Please don't do that!" Broke free, picked up my shoes, ran out the door, and walked home in my stocking feet. I was so upset at what happened that I had nightmares on being sexually assaulted by Art for weeks. Other men have courted me but all they did was hold my hand, no more. Art was cunning and sly and tried to maneuver me into a position so I would not say no because he wanted to satisfy his fleshly needs at my expense. Now, can we change the subject because it is very uncomfortable for me to talk about what Art tried to do to me."

George was embarrassed that he accused Cynthia of murdering Art, and asked, "Will you forgive me for thinking that you were a cold-blooded killer."

"Yes, I will."

"Would it bother you if I gave you a hug?"

"Matter of fact, I need one right now."

George held Cynthia in his arms, she slowly put her arms around him and said, "For some strange reason I feel comfortable and secure with you."

George let go of Cynthia a few minutes later and stated, "We have to clean this room up to get it ready for the Time Arch. Would it bother you if you put on one of my shirts and a pair of jeans? Because I would hate to see you get that pretty dress of yours dirty."

"Me, where men's trousers and a shirt? That'll be a first, I'll be right back."

Cynthia walked back in the lab 13 minutes later in a pair of man's jeans and a green plaid shirt. George stated, "Sweetheart, no matter what you wear you look beautiful. Now let's get to work and clean this dump."

Around 11:30 that evening Art Boulder's Bones were neatly tucked in a box, the gadget and tools on the table were placed in a bin in the barn and the table broke up for firewood.

George didn't have a problem setting up the Time Arch in the lab on the left wall, and the control console to the left of the arch.

Cynthia inquired, "Can you open the Arch anywhere?"

"Sure can. Why?"

"Could you open the arch over Center Hill Lake in Tennessee around midnight in 1850?"

George set the time coordinates, and stated, "The Arch is now opened over the center of the lake, did you wanna go for a midnight swim?"

Cynthia picked up the box that had Art's bones in it, stood in front of the Arch, and dumped the bones in the lake saying, "No one, but no one we'll find his bones there."

"I take it you were pretty ticked off at Art for what he tried to do to you."

"Hell, hath no fury like a woman scorned," stated Cynthia, "Now can you send me back to my home so I can make the preparations for our wedding?"

"I haven't even asked you to marry me yet."

"Yes, you have. Remember the flowers you gave me in the pasture earlier today and I told you that I would marry you."

'I'm sorry for being a little scatterbrained." George opened the Time Arch into a bedroom in Cynthia's cottage, held her in his arms and kissed her on the lips for the first time, and said, "I will see you in a week. Do you wanna get married in my time or yours?"

"Mine of course. Now get out of here you're not supposed to be in a woman's boudoir with her. But, before you go I want another kiss."

"Was that the first time a man ever kissed you on your lips?" George then gave Cynthia another kiss.

"Yes, it was, and thank you for the second kiss now get out of here before I stop being a proper woman."

3

An unwanted visitor

The next morning around six, George woke wondering, *"Is Cynthia telling me the truth that she didn't stab Art or is she pulling the wool over my eyes?"*

In his Time Lab under the barn, George set the Time Arch for three days before Cynthia met Art in June. put on old baggy pants over his regular clothes, disguised himself with long brown hair, mustache, beard, glasses, and an old ratty tan hat. Put an emergency Time Arch exit button in the heel of his shoe then exited the arch on a quiet stretch of the road that Cynthia's cottage was on. Six minutes later, George knocked on her front door. She opened it clad in a lacy pink gingham dress, smiled, and inquired, "Can I help you, Sir?"

"Could you give a poor man a few crumbs of bread that is down on his luck?"

"If you will sit in the wicker chair on the veranda I will see what I have to give you."

Cynthia came back 7 minutes later, placed a small black table in front of him, then sat a mug of hot coffee, a huge slice of apple pie, and a wedge of cheddar cheese. She sat in the wicker chair on his right and said, "I hope this is enough to hold you for a little while at least."

George bit into the wedge of cheese, and said, "I bet a pretty thing like you has to beat off the many beaus with a club."

"The last time I went with a beau was years ago. But I don't mind living by myself weighting for the right man to come along."

George then stated, "There are times when I want to stab someone for the way they treat me."

Poised in her chair, Cynthia stated, "I could never do anything like that. I remember some years back a man wanted to take me hunting. I told him no because I had to wear men's trousers and just the thought of killing a poor animal made me shutter."

George stared into her eyes and knew that she was telling him the truth.

Just then a short woman clad in a white blouse and a dark blue skirt that showed her ankles. Approached, stared at George, and said, "Getting kind of desperate with the guys aren't you."

"He's a good man who is down on his luck and I'm giving him something to eat. Enough with your crude remarks Ruth. Are you going to help me with the quilt or not?"

Ruth then stated boldly, "Hey, I know this really cute guy who is dying to date, somebody. What do you say? I can have him knocking on your door tomorrow."

Cynthia growled, "Can the garbage talk, my Saviour will provide me with a beau in His time."

Ruth took a bite of George's cheese, then questioned, "Hey, can I borrow your shoes? Mine has a nick in one heel and a button is missing on the left shoe and I want to impress this really cute guy."

Cynthia took off her shoes, gave them to her friend then put on Ruth's.

Ruth went to snitch a hunk of George's pie, he grabbed her hand saying, "You do that again and we're gonna have a come to Jesus meeting right here on the porch."

"My, aren't we the grouch."

"Oh, did I tell you that I am getting over a bad cold?" George then faked a cough.

Ruth nervously stared at George then quickly excused herself saying, "I'll get the sowing stuff out while you talk to your friend."

George finished his coffee, pie, and cheese then said, "Thank you for your kindness, it indeed has been a pleasure."

Cynthia gave George $25.00 saying, "Take this with my blessings."

George admired Ruth's horse and buggy as he left Cynthia's place, and some five miles down the road, he got rid of his old clothes and walked to Art's farm. He then entered the barn to check things out.

Art barged in shouting, "You have no business being in here now get out!"

George smiled and asked, "Do you still have your lab workshop underneath this barn?"

"What are you babbling about Mister?"

George grabbed the broomstick, shoved it in the hole in the floor, opening the trap door, then said, "That is what I am talking about."

"I am an inventor and I like to keep my inventions a secret, and how did you know about my hidden workshop?"

"I have my ways."

"I am trying to improve on the potato peeler, come up with a knife that a woman can use in the kitchen and men's underwear that doesn't have long legs."

"Ah yes, briefs, Ever thought about coming up with a small change purse that a woman can put in her handbag? Oh, just an off the wall question, Do you ever use your secret workshop to entertain women?"

"I sure do. Hey, let me show you the other things I have been working on."

In Art's workshop, George spotted a photo of Ruth sitting on the table by the cot and inquired, "Is she ever a looker! Your wife?"

"No just a very good friend,"

"Have you ever heard of someone by the name of Cynthia Atwater?"

"I sure have why do you ask?"

"Ohhh, just wondering because I have heard about her in my travels."

"I would like to come up with an invention that would convince her to give me some of her money."

"I thought she was just a lonely spinster struggling through life like the rest of us."

"Miss. Atwater's grandfather made his money selling liquor and her parents fell air to all that loot and they left it to her. However, I have a plan to bilk her of all that loot but just snuggling with her would suit me fine. Because I don't have the heart to be dishonest to a beautiful woman like Cynthia Atwater."

"Is there anything I can do to help? All I want is to enjoy the thrill of it."

"No, I just plan to court Cynthia with all kinds of sweet talk until she does whatever I want. Then when she is vulnerable I will give her a sob story so she will give me some money for my work."

Ruth entered the lab, saying, "Art my love. Cynthia takes a walk every day around two in the afternoon."

"Do we have to kill her?"

"Yes, now do as I say."

"Okay, I'll follow her and look for an opportunity to get to know her."

Ruth took a bone-handled hunting knife out of her handbag saying, "When you have Cyc's money, use this to get rid of her, then throw her body in the lake. Hey! what's he doing down here?"

"He's a fellow inventor and can be trusted."

"Are you sure about him?"

"Yes! I'm a good judge of character and I know when someone is lying to me."

After hearing Art talk about how he would get Cynthia's money out of her. George's anger burned within him and wanted to strangle Art right there in his lab. But he politely excused himself and headed back to Cynthia's place to tell her what Ruth had planned. Halfway there, George stopped and questioned within himself, *"If I tell Cynthia about Ruth and Art. How will that affect the timeline? Will she still be in love with me? Will I still be her knight in shining armor and save her from being murdered on the hauling road? I better go back home and plan for my wedding."*

Back in his own time, George studied the bone handle knife that was sticking in the corpse in the time lab and discovered that it was the same knife that Ruth gave Art. Then just out of curiosity, George did a search on the Internet for the history of miss Atwater and discovered that she was murdered in her sleep by an unknown assailant. He went to the police station and asked, "I Need the file on Cynthia Atwater's murder."

Some 7 minutes later, the clerk handed George the file and said, "Have fun solving this one."

He read, the night on August 10, 1890, Miss. Cynthia Atwater was stabbed to death in her bed. The body was so badly mutilated that it had to be a closed casket. There was no forced entry or struggle which means Miss Atwater was murdered in her sleep.

George took pictures of the report, handed it back then went home and set the Time Arch for midnight on August 10th. He slowly entered the Time Arch; the moonlight showed through the bedroom window and saw a shadowy figure approaching Cynthia lying in her bed sound asleep. He tackled the killer and they landed on the bed. Cynthia woke screaming as the two wrestled on top of her. The wood be killer sliced George's left arm and raced out of the bedroom. Cynthia pulled the string tied to her bedpost that turned on the light hanging from the ceiling in the middle of the room and inquired, "What's going on?"

"The same guy that tried to kill you on the hauling road just tried it again."

Cynthia exclaimed, "Good Lord, you're left arm is bleeding!" She jumped out of bed in her long cotton bright yellow nightgown that had lace around the neck, cuffs, and hem.

George commented, "Nice nighty."

"Never mind me, I have to bandage that arm of yours."

After his arm was bandaged, Cynthia put on her thin light blue robe, made a pot of tea, cut some slices from a fresh loaf of gingerbread, sat at the dark wooden kitchen table, and asked, "How did you know that I was going to be attacked?"

"I searched the internet and discovered that you were murdered in your sleep. Then I went to the police to get the report."

"What did the police report say? if you don't mind me asking."

"It said that your body was so badly mutilated that it had to be a closed casket. Which tells me that someone is out for revenge."

Cynthia took a sip of her cold tea, stared at George, then got up, went into the next room, came back with a drawing pad and a pencil. She sat down and sketched the face of a man who had long hair, beard, glasses, and a tattered hat. She showed it to George and asked, "Does he look familiar?"

George chuckled then stated, "You're one smart cookie. How did you know it was me?"

"When I served you the cheese and pie, I noticed your brown shoes, then when I was tending to the wound on your arm you were wearing the same shoes. That's when I realized that you went back in time to check on me. You care to explain your actions?"

"I wasn't snooping on you honestly."

"Then what were you doing if you weren't checking up on me. Do you think I lied to you when I told you that I didn't stab Art."

"I wasn't sure if you were telling me the truth or what. Give me a break, I've only known you for a day."

Cynthia growled, "Why don't you stop beating around the bush and come right out and tell me that I'm a cold-blooded killer."

"I, I wasn't sure and I needed some proof that you are the kind, sweet, gentle, loving woman that I fell in love with."

"Oh, so now you're buttering me up to get on my good side."

"I give up, if you don't want me around just say so and I'll go back through the Time Arch that is still open in your bedroom and leave you alone."

Cynthia sat in George's lap, put her arms around his neck, kissed him then stated, "My life would be so boring without you, and just remember our wedding is only a few days away."

Cynthia made a fire in the old fashion kitchen wood stove, filled a large chrome tea kettle with water, then when the water was boiling, she poured the hot water in a fancy flowered teapot, added loose tea leaves, and waited for it to steep before pouring themselves a cup of tea,

George stated. "About 18 years from now in 1908 somebody is going to invent the teabag." Took a swallow of his tea and stated, "I assume after Knoxville, Tennessee had their first power station on December 1885 a few years later your community was wired for electricity."

"Yes, I see you've done your homework. You stay here and finish your tea while I go upstairs and put something decent on."

"Sweet, It's 7 o'clock in the morning. Why don't you go back to bed and I'll stand guard."

George found a Winchester rifle In the kitchen closet, sat in the living room with it across his lap, and went to sleep.

At ten that morning, he was suddenly stirred from his slumber by a man in his mid-40s wearing coveralls. Banged on the kitchen wall and shouted, "Cynthia, get your lazy hide out of bed and make me some breakfast!"

George stood in the kitchen doorway, leveled the Winchester rifle at him, and stated, "Mister. I don't know who you are but, you do not come in this house in order Cynthia around. Now go back out that door or I'll ventilate your head right where you stand."

Cynthia rushed into the kitchen while tying her bathrobe and question, "Was that Don Hollister I just heard?"

"Yes, and I threw him out. Because he has no business barging in this house without knocking. Especially when you're in bed sleeping."

"Don has always ordered me around and I've never had the courage to stand up to him and tell him no. There have been times where he came into my bedroom early in the morning, pulled me out of bed in my nightclothes so I could make breakfast for him. But I never had the courage to tell him not to come in my home when I am in bed."

"I know you're a kind trusting woman but from now on, lock your doors when you go to bed so he doesn't barge in on you."

Cynthia gave George a kiss and said, "Have I told you lately that I love you and thank you for standing up to Don."

George went out the back door and told Don, "Cynthia isn't properly dressed right now so sit on the front veranda and I will bring your bacon and eggs out to you, and if you ever barge in this house again I'll throw you right through the door, do I make myself clear?"

"Who are you and what gives you the right to be in her house when she's not properly dressed?" demanded Don.

"The one who will be marrying Cynthia in a few days. So, from here on in, go someplace else for your free food because your days of pushing Cynthia around are over."

On the front veranda, Don repeatedly pounded his finger on Georgia's chest saying, "Cynthia and I go way back to when we were just kids. We went swimming together In the old swimming hole and did all kinds of crazy things when we were growing up. So, you are not going to tell me what I can and cannot do with her. Since Cynthia has been making me breakfast for the past 20 years, she will continue to make it whether you like it or not."

"You're lying through your teeth and you know it. Cynthia is a modest Cristian woman and would never have gone swimming alone with any boy, especially you. Now eat your breakfast, leave, and don't come back." roared George.

"Oh, and by the way I'm marrying Cynthia not you," stated Don in a firm voice.

Cynthia walked out on the front verandah clad in a white blouse in a deep blue skirt that went down to her ankles, and stated, "Stop telling lies about me, Don. I never went swimming with you or did any crazy things and surely I am not going to be marrying you. Now finish your breakfast and please leave and don't bother coming back tomorrow morning for food because I will not answer the door."

"You mean I won't be able to see you in that tiny cute frilly thing you wear to bed."

An enraged Cynthia screamed, "I don't have a tiny cute frilly anything and no man has ever seen me bare-naked at any time so stop lying!"

George grabbed Don by the back of his shirt and the seat of his pants and threw him off the property.

With Don gone, Cynthia stated, "I am so glad he is out of my life. I'm sorry I didn't tell you about him but that guy has been spreading all kinds of rumors around about me that I'm too embarrassed to tell you."

"Did Don ever force himself on you in bed?"

"Thank the Lord, no. But he has barged in my home and saw me in my nightclothes more times than I care to remember. Now can we change the subject? I would like to take you into town and show you around then take you to the prayer meeting tonight."

"Is Don the reason why you stay by yourself a lot?"

"Yes, If I go into town and he sees me. I become his slave for the rest of the day. Going here, going there, fetching this, fetching that. I swear that guy is the laziest human on 2 feet. Always looking for people to do things for him. Oh, there was this one time he wanted to give me a back rub and put his hands on my shoulders. I spun around and slapped him in the face which totally shocked him. But he never asked me to do that again."

"Do all your nightgowns come down to your feet?"

"Yes, of course, all the nightwear are like that in the 1890s." Cynthia hugged George and questioned, "Do I detect some jealousy in the tone of your voice? Don is the only man that has seen me in my nightclothes and those times were against my wishes. No, I was never romantically involved with any man that saw more of me than he should have. I love you and I have no desire to look any further. So, you can put your jealousy away."

4

Time line shocker

Instead of taking her horse and buggy, Cynthia fired up her Curtis Steamer automobile and drove to Knoxville with George and the two of them had lunch at a sidewalk café. She took a swallow of her lemonade, handed George a list of toys she wanted to buy for the curio shop in his time.

He stared at the list, and stated, "I see you are a regular entrepreneur."

"I have to make money to keep the home fires burning." Stated Cynthia.

"I wasn't going to mention this but what about all that money your parents left you from your grandfather's alcohol business? Did you spend it all? Did Art con you out of all that loot?"

Cynthia made as if she didn't hear George, and stated, "I can't wait to see Francis's face when I bring that list of items into her shop."

George questioned, "Are you embarrassed to say that you lost your parent's inheritance?"

Cynthia hung her head and stated, "Shortly after I walked out on Art, I went to the First Bank of Tennessee to withdraw some money. And they told me my account had a zero balance. I asked him how can that be? My grandfather opened that account years ago. He left it to my parents who left it to me now you're telling me there's nothing in it?"

The bank teller stated, "You came in one day last week wearing a blue checkered calico dress with matching hat, withdrew all your money, and left with your boyfriend Arthur."

Fortunately, my father stashed a good chunk of that money behind a loose rock in the basement wall and that's what I've been living on."

George caught the waiter's attention and ordered two hamburgers with lettuce, tomato, onion, relish, and catch up on Kaiser rolls. He looked at Cynthia, held her hands, and stated, "I could easily go back in time and you could withdraw that money but Art is a slippery little bugger and would find another way to steal your money. But It's my fault just as much as it is yours. I went back in time just before you met Art and talk to him and his lab and knew he was planning to romance you just to get your money. However, if I would've told you then, we would not be sitting here having this conversation today because the timeline would have changed. But, the question I have is who has the money? Did Ruth stab Art, frame you, and take off with the money. Or did you and Ruth kill Art because he stole your money, left him in his workshop in the lab under the barn knowing that no one would find him."

George took a bite of his hamburger, then inquired, "What is it that you're not telling me? How did Art con you out of your money? Was it through sweet talk? Did he blackmail you?"

"Art came to my house late one afternoon with some venison and told me that he wanted to cook me a fabulous meal, which he did. After that meal and a hearty slice of apple pie, I was stuffed and fell asleep on the divan. I woke around 10 o'clock that night, Art was gone, and so were the papers that told everything about my grandfather's fortune. It was the very next day in his lab under the barn Art tried to force me into doing something that was immorally wrong. But how Art knew where those papers were, I never told him and the only rooms he was in was the kitchen, and the parlor where we sat, drank tea, and talked, and no we did not kiss if that's what you're thinking."

"Your friend Ruth was working with Art. Her job was to be buddy buddies with you so she could pump you for information without you knowing it. After a while, I assume you trusted her and Ruth had free reign of the house to check for the papers or anything that would tell her where the money was."

Just then, Ruth sauntered bye wearing a very expensive dress from Saks Fifth Avenue. She sat at the table with Cynthia and George, smiled politely, and stated, "I haven't seen you since you fed that bum on your front veranda. How are you doing? I heard from a friend of mine that the bank lost all your money, I am so sorry." Ruth gazed at George, quickly rubbed his back, and said, "Just don't tell anybody what we did after you left Art's lab." Ruth stared at Cynthia and stated, "Oh I'm sorry, I forgot you were here."

Cynthia wanted to slap that silly smile off Ruth's face because she knew where she got the money to buy that expensive dress. She knew that George was faithful to her and Ruth was trying to make her jealous. However, Cynthia stated with a forced smile, "Good for you, I'm glad things are going your way, talk to you later."

After Ruth had left, Cynthia stared at George and growled, "When are you going to stop accusing me of being the killer?"

"With all the clues in Art's lab pointing to you as the murderer and Don coming into your home early in the morning has me wondering."

Cynthia's face grew dark as she stated, "In other words, you think I killed Art and I'm running around the house butt naked with Don having sex with him every morning."

George smiles sheepishly and asked, "Well aren't you?"

An enraged Cynthia stated, "That's it, one more word out of you Mister and we are through!"

"What would you think if you were in my shoes?"

"Four one, I would polish them more often, and I would exercise some faith."

George pondered carefully about what he was going to say next then stated, "In my time it's difficult to find a 26-year-old woman that has never been in bed with a man."

Cynthia stared at George in silence then stated, "You're kidding. Aren't you?"

"No, I am not and I can prove it to you if you want me to."

"Alright, but first we buy the things on my list than we go back to your time so you can show me."

Later that day, they entered the toy store and bought several stuffed teddy bears, stuffed cats, several dolls of different sizes, small horses mounted on wooden platforms with wheels, a Choo, Choo train that a boy could pull around. From there they went to the jewelry store and Cynthia bought several earrings and a couple of brooches.

Back in George's time, Cynthia inquired, "George Babe. Can you open a portal anywhere?"

"Yeah. Why."

"Then opened a Time Arch in Ruth's bedroom, here is her address, the time should be two in the morning,"

"What are you going to do Cynthia?"

Cynthia smiled devilishly and stated, "I can't tell you."

George opened a Time Arch to Ruth's coordinates, Cynthia rushed through coming back five minutes later with Ruth's dress from Saks Fifth Avenue.

George gazed at the expensive dress and stated, "That is stealing."

"Not really, seeing that she bought it with my money."

"You don't know that."

"Ruth works as a cashier at the Great Atlantic and Pacific Tea Company and makes just enough money to get by and lives in a dingy apartment."

"I see what you are saying but it is still wrong." George chuckled and said, "You are a spiteful little thing, aren't you."

Later, Cynthia entered France's Curio Shop with George, opened her paper shopping bag, and showed her what she had.

Frances was thrilled when she saw the toys, but, when Cynthia put the jewelry from 1890 on the counter, Francis became overly excited and had to sit down. She then asked, "Where in the world did you get these treasures? They're worth a fortune."

Cynthia smiled then stated, "Here is a dress from Saks Fifth Avenue, put this in your window and people will beat a path to your door."

"You are kidding me! This dress is priceless and here I was about to close my shop because nobody was buying my stuff."

George reached in his pocket, pulled out a $20 bill that Cynthia gave him in 1890, and said, "This should bring in a collector or two."

"I already know somebody that was looking for a bill like this, thank you."

George then drove to Inskip Pool and Park, escorted Cynthia to the poolside. She stared at the men and women around the Olympic size swimming pool and stated, "Men and women bathing to gather? That's disgusting and look at them they are hardly dressed!" Cynthia pointed to a young woman and commented, "That young lady by the diving board in pink. She is almost bare-naked and most of her derrière is exposed."

George chuckled and said, "She is wearing a string bikini."

Cynthia's face suddenly turned red from embarrassment and quickly spun around and asked, "Babe, can we leave? I've seen more than I wanted to."

"What's wrong?"

"Never mind, let's just go back to the automobile if you please."

"Oh, You mean the tall well-built man that just got on the diving board wearing the blue Speedo, bothers you?"

"Yes, and I am not used to seeing a man with so little clothes on, now let's go, please."

In the car, Cynthia gazed at George and said, "I understand why you would suspect me and Don messing around. People in my time wouldn't even think of wearing those few pieces of cloth they call a bathing suit. Plus, the morals in your time are loose compared to the 1890s. In my time, men would never think about swimming with women, and as you know the bathing suits in my time cover the entire body and are loose-fitting. This way a man or a woman can't get excited staring at someone's exposed body. I guess this is what you would call a timeline shocker."

"I think it's time I introduce you to a shopping mall, then we can go back to your time and attend the Wednesday night prayer meeting at your church."

"It's a deal."

George drove to the Pinnacle at Turkey Creek shopping mall, Open the car door for Cynthia, held her hand, and entered the immense mall. The vastness of the building and a mob of people rushing in and out of stores almost overwhelmed her.

Cynthia stated, "This is one huge store."

"Actually, there is a large number of stores under this roof. That's why they call it a mall. You wanna have a cup of coffee in Starbucks?"

"Sure, why not."

As they were approaching the coffee shop, a man in his early thirties, clad in dirty jeans and a gray sweatshirt, raced out of a store carrying a black leather purse and a woman was screaming, "That man just stole my pocketbook!"

George took chase and tackled him in front of the IMAX, gave the woman her purse, and handed the man to the mall security.

A frightened Cynthia held George's right arm and inquired, "Is your time overrun with gangsters and why are all the people's clothing so tight? Don't they have the money to buy clothes that fit?"

"It's the style."

Shocked at what she saw, Cynthia asked, "You mean that woman coming out of that store with the green top and black pants that are so tight you can see everything she has. Is the style?"

"Yes, a lot of women wear that type of pants."

"In my time, that woman would be arrested for indecent exposure and don't expect me to dress like that because I won't."

George smiled and said, "If you start to wear clothes that accent your figure, I will lay my hands on you and pray for you."

In Starbucks, George walked up to the counter and ordered two coffees. The man behind him approached the counter and shouted, "This coffee is cold and I asked for peppermint coffee not regular!"

The young woman behind the counter stated politely, "I am truly sorry for the mix-up Sir, but I can't do anything now because you drank most of the coffee."

"Then I demand to see the manager!"

George took the man's coffee, placed it on the counter, stuffed a ten-dollar bill in his shirt pocket, and said, "Go complain someplace else."

The man walked away grumbling, "It would have to snow in July before I come in here again."

"Fine with me," muttered the young woman behind the counter.

George sat at a round table with Cynthia and she stated, "I believe you now but, you are not from Tennessee, are you."

"No, I am from Holyoke, Massachusetts. In 2010 my wife Betty and I bought a white raised ranch just north of Holyoke. Two weeks after we moved into our fabulous home. I came home from work and found my wife sitting on the couch with her head down. I asked, "Betty, what's wrong?"

She said, "I'm having a private Bible study with Frank because his wife threw him out of the house, but that's all right I can handle things."

I told her, "That is not right having him here when I am not home. Besides the Word of God says to abstain from all appearances of evil."

A week or two later, my wife was going out on dates with Frank and I suspected that they were satisfying each other's flesh in bed. But I couldn't prove it. However, I came home from work a month later, found the living room area rug messed up, and my wife in bed with Frank. She promptly got out of bed and threw me out of the house and I lost my home, job, wife, and everything. Fortunately, Betty didn't get the $500,000.00 I had stuffed in a Wells Fargo Bank Savings account. So, I bought a car, drove down to Tennessee, and bought the farm, built the Time Arch, and began to sell Antiques from 1890. That's when I decided to look for a main squeeze. I discovered a woman was murdered on the hauling road in 1890, went back in time and rescued you."

Cynthia thought for a minute and stated, "I figure Betty was a Christian. If so, how did she convince your pastor that she was innocent?"

"Betty told the pastor that she caught me in our living room with just my bath towel on, locked in a passionate embrace with our maid. Which was a lie? But the pastor believed her instead of me."

Cynthia took a swallow of her coffee, then inquired, "What about the time you went to borrow a loaf of bread from your wife's friend Mandy who lived next-door? What did you do when you entered her house?"

A shocked George questioned, "How did you find out about Mandy?"

"I read your journal and it was vague concerning her."

"It went like this. One evening my wife Betty asked, "George Honey, could you go next door and borrow a loaf of bread from Mandy? I don't have enough for our pick-nick tomorrow."

Next door, George rang the doorbell, Mandy, a 20-year-old woman with short light brown hair opened the door in a short thin blue nighty and said smiling, "Come in and weight until I get the bread."

I sensed a setup and said, "I'll wait outside thank you."

"When I got back with the bread, Betty screamed, "You should be ashamed of yourself being lewd around poor Mandy!"

"I tried to explain to my wife that I didn't go in but she wouldn't listen to me,"

Cynthia stated, "Betty set you up so she could have an excuse to divorce you."

George chuckled and said, "You know it. However, everybody, I knew thought that I was going to end my marriage by going to bed with Mandy. But Betty wound up sleeping with Frank, Mandy's boyfriend's brother."

Cynthia finished her coffee and asked, "Can we go home now? I've had enough timeline shockers for today."

5

A change in time

At the old white Pentecostal church that was close to the hauling road south of Knoxville, Tennessee in1890. George spoke to Pastor Tumwater after the Wednesday night prayer meeting saying, "Have you heard that whatever you need as a child of God can be found in the Cross of Jesus Christ?"

"No, but please explain."

"It's not the wooden structure that Christ died on but what He did on the Cross. When Christ said, 'It is finished,' Salvation was provided to all mankind. That means whatever the Child of God needs healing, deliverance, a new job, a car, even a wife has been provided through the finished work on the cross. All the person has to do is receive it by faith the way they received Christ when they first were saved."

"You mean that I don't have to have all kinds of faith to be healed of Cancer, but claim it by faith through the finished work on the Cross?"

"Yes, if you have to fast and pray for something you need in Christ it is dead works."

"I see, it is not what I can do it's what Christ has done on the Cross. Whoa, whoa! That's gonna make a huge difference in my relationship with my Saviour. Thanks, Brother. Oh, are you and Cynthia ready for your wedding in two days?" Pastor Tumwater Gazed at Cynthia holding onto George's right arm and stated, "I have never seen her look happier."

George's fancy black wristwatch caught on the sleeve of his suit coat jacket. The Pastor spotted it, took hold of his arm, and asked softly, "Would you please explain to me what this is?"

Cynthia stared at George and said, "I think you should tell him."

A puzzled Pastor questioned, "Tell me what?"

George quickly glanced around and asked, "Is there a place where we can talk?"

The Pastor brought George and Cynthia through a door on the left side of the platform and into his office. Sat behind his desk and said, "Now tell me."

George smiled sheepishly and said, "I am from the year 2020, and I came back in time to save Cynthia from being brutally murdered. Here's my driver's license and birth certificate. Oh, a man by the name of Bill Waters will come by tomorrow and hand you five hundred dollars for the roof repairs,"

The Pastor stated calmly, "I am still not convinced that you are a time traveler."

George reached in his side pocket showed Pastor Tumwater his smart iPhone and stated, "This is the telephone in my time." He accessed the color photos on the phone and had the pastor leaf through them.

A short time later, the Pastor handed the iPhone back to George and inquired. "Could you tell me what Is going to happen to my church in the future?"

"I could, but that would change the timeline and possibly ruin some blessings that the Lord has in store for you. So, my advice is to seek the Lord Jesus and he will guide you."

"Are you two sure you are ready for your wedding this Wednesday? Because you haven't had your rehearsal yet. have you picked out the bridesmaids in best man?"

Cynthia stated, "I know I have been a little scatterbrained when you've asked me to do things around the church in the past but everything is ready to go so don't worry."

The pastor stared at George and said, "Time Traveler, if I were you, I would lose the watch and your picture phone before someone sees them and they get you in big trouble." The pastor sat back in his chair, smiled, and stated, "You have just given me an idea for this Sunday sermon. 'Christ, the ultimate time traveler." Mankind set his course through time for destruction when he disobeyed the Lord in the garden. Since heaven is outside of time, our Savior can see mankind's entire life and can choose any point in his life to intervene. Christ entered our linear timeline and changed mankind's course from destruction to glory."

"Good ideas. Thank you, Pastor, from now on I'll leave my watch and cell phone at home. Cynthia, we have to leave."

Back in George's time, Cynthia walked in the living room clad in a blue printed calico that went down to her knees, twirled around in front of George, and asked, "Is this the kind of clothing that is acceptable in your time?"

"Yes, and you look great."

I am used to wearing two kinds of underliners, along with a structural garment, a corset along with thigh high stockings and a dress that covers all of me, except my head and hands. This getup makes me feel like I am in the buff. So, if you don't mind, I am gonna wear my usual clothing until I get used to wearing almost nothing compared to the 1890s clothing."

"That's fine with me. But what timeline do you want to live in?"

"With you in this timeline silly. True, most of the clothing in your timeline looks like it's been painted on the person and the morals here are almost non-existent. But I think we can make a difference for Christ."

On the day of the wedding, the church that was situated 300 yards from a hauling road south of Knoxville, Tennessee in 1890 was packed with guests, George wore a black tuxedo and Cynthia wore a modest white lacy wedding gown. After the wedding, the reception was held on the church side lawn. During the reception, Cynthia whispered in George's ear, "Just wait until I get you alone tonight Mister."

Ruth hid in the crowd, took out her Pocket Kodak Camera and took a picture of George and Cynthia, then quickly left.

Close to the end of the reception, a horse-drawn patty wagon stopped in front of the church, two police officers got off and walked up to Cynthia. One of them stated, "We've been looking for you for a long time. Cynthia Celestina Atwater, you are under arrest for the murder of Art Boulder."

George stood in front of the police officer and asked, "Wait a minute, what evidence do you have that my wife murdered Art? Do you have the murder weapon? Can you produce his body?"

"A woman reported that her boyfriend Art was missing, I went to his farm and found a bloody knife, shirt, and evidence that Miss Atwater is the killer."

George stated, "I own that farm now, and the 4th Amendment that was added to the Bill of Rights on December 15, 1791, protects people from the police searching their homes and private property without a search warrant."

"We have been to Miss. Atwater for a long time, now we have her."

"Why didn't you just go to her house and arrest her back then instead of waiting until now?"

The other police officer pushed George to one side stating, "Step aside Sir, you're interfering in police business."

George suspected that the police officers were frauds and figured that someone was going to great lengths to get Cynthia out of the way. He stared at the officers and pleaded, "My wife has to use the little house out back before you put her in the Patty Wagon. Oh, I have to be in there to help her because of her disability."

The officer with silent for a few seconds then said, "Alright but don't try any funny business."

As George escorted his wife to the outhouse that was 20 feet in back of the church, she whispered, "What are you talking about, I don't have to pee?"

"I have a plan."

In the outhouse, George sat on the seat while Cynthia stood in front of him. He took off his left shoe, remove the Emergency Time Arch Button that was concealed in the heal, held onto his wife, and tumbled through the arch back to his time.

George sat in his brown easy chair in his living room, glanced at his watch and stated, "If we leave now, we can get to the police station in time to do a search for your arrest warrant back in 1890. And if it's not there then will know that those guys that were trying to arrest you wear hired by someone."

Cynthia sat on the floor next to George, unbuttoned her shoes and stated Softly, "The wedding and reception took a lot out of me, so, why don't we go upstairs to the bedroom and cuddle for a bit."

"In other words, going to the police station can wait."

"Yes, and I need in my life right now, and that is you."

"You get no argument from me let's go upstairs."

At 10 after 7 the next morning, Cynthia sat on the left side of the bed, and stated, "I don't believe we spent 12 hours in bed."

George rubbed her bareback and questioned, "Are you complaining?"

"I'm just surprised that's all. Now let me throw some clothes on so I can make us some breakfast."

Cynthia took her light blue bra and underwear out of the top dresser drawer from Georges' time, looked at them, and said, "I might as well get used to wearing so little foundation garments. Sweetheart, could you hand me my blue calico dress from the closet?"

That afternoon, Cynthia dressed in a long-sleeve yellow blouse and a long dark blue skirt and said, "I don't feel naked in this outfit the way I did in that thin blue calico dress."

George took her to town to a mall so she could buy some clothes. She was able to buy 6 pairs of string tied pantaloons underwear and several up to date foundation garments. While she was looking at some dishes, a man in his forties walked up to her and stuck a knife in her side saying, "You are gonna take me to an ATM where you are going to withdraw whatever is in your account."

"What is an ATM?"

He added pressure to the knife saying, "Don't get cute with me lady. Now move."

As Cynthia approached the store's mall entrance with the man, George hollered, "Cynthia, where are you going?" As he spotted the knife in the man's hand. The thug spun around with Cynthia saying, "Just keep walking Mister."

George stated, "You know it is a miracle that someone hasn't fainted in this sweltering heat," glanced down at the thug's foot, then at his wife. She came down hard on his toes with her heal. He screamed in pain as George, grabbed the knife, spun him around, and stuck it in his chest.

The attacker stared at the knife in him in shock, then collapsed on the floor dead. Later in Starbucks, a scared Cynthia sat at a round table with George trying to keep her hand from shaking. Took a swallow of her black robust coffee and asked, "Is it always this dangerous shopping in your time?"

"No, Sometimes it's worse." quipped George. "Why just last week some crazed maniac ran through the mall slashing people with his machete. Do you still want to live in my time?"

"More than ever, and that fictitious machete guy doesn't scare me."

Just then a tall thin woman in her thirties clad in jeans and a blue t-shirt sat next to Cynthia and said, "Do you know that you resemble my great-great grandmother's friend. My name is Ruthie, here let me show you a photo of my great-great-grandmother." She then showed a photo of Cynthia and Ruth standing in front of her cottage.

Cynthia inquired, "Did your great-great-grandmother tell you anything about her friend?"

"Bundles, she told me that Cynthia stabbed her friend's Art in the chest then hit his body. She also told me that Cynthia had a diamond-shaped mole on her left forearm and the big toe on her right foot is smaller than the one on her left."

Ruthie took out another photo from her black leather purse and said, "This is the only picture of Cynthia when she married her husband, George."

Ruthie stared at George and Cynthia then at the picture and exclaimed, "Oh my gosh! I have never seen this in all the years I've been researching ancestors. Cynthia, you and your husband are an exact duplicate of my great-great, grandmother's friend, and her husband, plus you 2 have the same names." Ruthie studied the mole on the left side of George's face, looked at the photo, and asked, "How can 2 people look exactly like a couple that lived 130 years ago? I know there is no such thing as time travel, by any chance are you 2 clones?"

Cynthia cuddled up to George and stated, "We're just a young married couple in love that happened to look like somebody in the past."

George asked, "Could somebody have used photoshop to doctor up the pictures?"

"No!" stated Ruthie in a stern voice. "I was with my grandmother when she took the photos out of an old dusty box in her attic. Then she showed me the pocket Kodak Camera that my great-great-grandmother used to take the pictures with. Now if you'll excuse me I have to go home and do some more research because this is way too weird and I'll see you 2 later."

Close to three o'clock George entered the police station with his wife and asked to look through their archives.

The clerk stated, "You again. Did you solve that last murder or are you working on a new one?"

"The Same one."

"Help yourself."

In the basement of the police department hours later, Cynthia stated, "Hey I found an arrest warrant for Ruth. It seems that she was arrested for robbing a bank but her conviction was overturned."

"Good. Make a copy of that and this one that says that Art was reported missing by a woman named Ruthie White." Stated George.

Cynthia's eyes widened as she read an arrest warrant for Pastor Tumwater's wife for shooting her husband for cheating on her." Then gave it to her husband to read. George studied the report that said, "Your friend Ruth accused Pastor of sexually assaulting her one afternoon."

"Pastor would never do anything like that. He loves his wife Kathy very much. Does it give a date that it was supposed to take place?"

"Yup, it happened on Saturday, November 12, 1892."

"Can we stop by the old church? I want to see what it looks like today."

Later, George stopped his car in front of the old Pentecostal church that was boarded up. Cynthia rushed up to the church, ripped off the boards across the door, and ran inside and fell at the alter crying. George sat on the floor on her right side and inquired, "Are you alright?"

"I will be in a minute." She then dried her eyes and asked, "Can we go back in time and prevent this from happening?"

"I don't know. I do not like deliberately changing the timeline"

"Please, Hon."

"Okay. Let's go home and change the timeline."

In the time lab, George set the Time Arch for November 12, 1892, then walked through it holding his wife's hand.

They exited the arch between two large fir trees just off the hauling road. Several hundred feet from the church, Cynthia saw the Pastor working on the front steps and energetically waved shouting, "Hi Pastor!"

He put his hammer down, took a swallow of his iced tea, and questioned, "What brings you, two newlyweds, here on such a lovely Saturday afternoon?"

George sat on the steps and stated, "You are going to council Ruth today aren't you."

"Why yes. She is supposed to be here in a half-hour. Is there something going to happen that I should know?"

"It's a setup. Ruth is going to accuse you of sexually assaulting her, your wife will find out and shoot you for being unfaithful. She will be hung for killing you and the church will fold and will be abandon."

George then showed Pastor Tumwater the police report as Ruth approached the Pastor clad in her Sunday finest. She smiled at Cynthia and said, "You will have to excuse us, the Pastor, and I have business to discuss."

Cynthia got in Ruth's face and stated, "You are a backstabbing weasel. I know you found where my money was being kept and that you are trying to blame me for killing Art. But it won't work. I also know what you plan to accuse the Pastor of doing during your so-called counseling session today. But you are not going to close this church By dragging pastor Tumwater through the mud and close this church through false accusations."

In mock innocence, Ruth stated, "You have it all wrong, I'm here for counseling that's all and I'm surprised at your accusations after we've been such good friends."

George held his wife around her waist and questioned, "Who is it that is paying you to frame Pastor Tumwater? Oh, just to let you know. I'll know if you try to bother the Pastor again. So, crawl back under that rock that you came from."

An upset Ruth spun around on her heels and stormed off.

The pastor thanked George and Cynthia for saving him from a serious problem and invited them to supper.

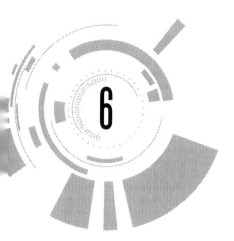

6

The game's afoot

Some two weeks later, George opened a red notebook on his mahogany desk, saw a bunch of numbers before his wife's log entry, and shouted, "Cynthia, can you come here for a minute?"

She walked up behind him, kissed him on his left cheek, and questioned, "What's bugging you?"

"What are those numbers before each entry in your journal?"

"I'm keeping track of what time we went and the date. The numbers after Kansas City, 09101890-1000A means that we were in Kansas City, Kansas on September 9th, 1890 at ten AM. By keeping track of where and when it saves us from running into each other in future excursions."

"Very good idea."

"I think it's time we went to my place 2 weeks after our wedding in 1890 and pack my things and bring them to your place."

"Get the raincoats because it is pouring outside,"

Cynthia brought her husband in the basement, tilted an old large book on the brown bookshelf forward. The bookshelf slowly swung open revealing a dark tunnel to the barn.

"Whoa! Spider city!" stated George, "Get a broom so we can clear some of those cobwebs."

Cynthia brushed them aside saying, "Scared of a little spider?"

"When the spider has his whole family and relatives in one spot. Yes!"

"Arachnophobia?" asked Cynthia.

"You know it."

"Here, let me hold your hand and we'll go through the tunnel together."

"When we finish cleaning your cottage, I am gonna use a case of bug spray on this tunnel, vacuum them up and burn them in the fireplace."

At Cynthia's cottage two weeks after their wedding in1890. She sold the furniture in the living room, dining room, the beds, and some of the pots and pans in the kitchen. Cynthia piled all her clothes on the back of a horse-drawn wagon that they borrowed from Herman their neighbor along with some of the food in the kitchen and headed for George's farm in 1890 with him driving Cynthia's car that was parked in the barn.

A tall lanky man In his late 50s, dressed in coveralls by the name of Herman was bringing the last of Cynthia's clothes in the house and offered her 35,000 dollars cash for her cottage. Late that afternoon, the papers for the sale of the house were signed, Cynthia had the money in her hands, went in the basement, removed a rock in the cellar wall and took out a canvas bag full of money and deposited it in Wells Fargo bank along with the money from the sale of the house.

Back in 2020, Cynthia and George carried her belongings through the Time Arch and put them in one of the spare bedrooms upstairs. As George and his wife were relaxing in the living room with a mug of coffee, the front doorbell rang. George answered it. Ruthie pushed her way in and demanded, "Just who are you two?"

"My wife told you in Starbucks that we are two people very much in love. Would you like a mug of coffee while we sit and talk?"

In the living room, Ruthie Set on a couch from 1890, took a swallow of her coffee, placed it on the coffee table from the 1800s, and stated, "After doing more research I decided that you two are time travelers."

George stared at Ruthie and asked, "What have you been smoking? Time travelers? Yeah, right."

Ruthie took another swallow of her coffee and said, "George, I like your shoes. Kinda like the ones the George in 1890 is wearing. Oh, just to let you know. There is no birth record of a Cynthia Celestina Atwater borne in or around Knoxville, Tennessee for the last 120 years."

Cynthia served fresh chewy Brownies that she baked earlier, Ruthie took a bite of her Brownie and said, "I like soft chewy ones. Thank you."

She gazed at George and said, "Your family the Bentwoods, came to America from England in the late 1700s and settled in North Dakota. In 1937 the Bentwoods moved to Massachusetts where you are from. There is no record of any Bentwood in Tennessee. Then poof, in 1890 for a brief few days they show up, you and your wife to be exact. All the evidence says that you two are time travelers, however, there is no way a body can travel through time. Or can they?"

George gazed at his wife as if to say, *"What do we do now? Do we tell her about the Time Arch?"*

Cynthia silently took Ruthie's right hand, lead her into the basement and opened the tunnel then brought her into the time lab and showed her the dimly lit Time Arch bathed in a pale blue light.

George asked, "Ruthy, Where would you like to go in time?"

"I knew it!" shouted Ruthie, "I would like to meet my great-great-grandmother, Ruth."

George set the Time Arch for Knoxville, Tennessee, Saturday, July11, at two in the afternoon in 1891. The Time Arch glowed a bright blue, as they entered.

That Saturday was high in the nineties as they sat at a round metal table at a sidewalk café and George ordered strawberry ice cream floats for everyone.

Ruthie inquired, "Why is everyone staring at me?"

Cynthia smiled and said, "Women your age in 1891 do not wear tattered jeans and a t-shirt."

George pointed to a well-dressed slender woman approaching and said, "That is your great-great-grandmother."

Ruth sat next to George, gazed at Ruthie's torn jeans and t-shirt, and questioned, "Who's the grunge ball?"

"She's a friend." stated Cynthia.

"Feeding another lowlife again I see."

Ruth briskly rubbed George's right arm and inquired, "So, how is married life treating you? Have any kids yet?" Ruth then stared at Ruthie and stated, "For some reason, you give me the creeps. It's as if I am looking at myself."

Ruthie stated, "I hear that you had a baby boy by Arthur Boulder. Is that true? Did you give it up for adoption, and are the parents asking for child support? Is that true? I also heard that you robbed a bank but it was overturned."

Ruth nervously stared at Ruthie but did not want to answer for fear that she may say something that would give away her secret.

Ruthie then stated, "I heard that your sudden riches were ill-gotten. Is that true?"

Ruth's eyes bulged as her face turned red with anger, picked up Ruthie's ice cream, dumped it on her head, and stormed off.

Ruthie wiped off the ice cream saying, "That wasn't very nice of her. I expected that my great-great-grandmother would be sweet and gentle."

Cynthia stated sarcastically, "Ruth, Sweet, Gentle? She is a sly weasel that has a bad attitude."

"Can we go back now? I've seen enough."

George inquired, "Ruthie, how are you at solving murders?"

"I love trying to figure out who don it."

"Excellent, I have a good one for you."

At Georges farm in 1891, he brought Ruthie and his wife into the time lab under the barn and showed her the corpse of Art Boulder.

Ruthie stated, "A murder in time, I love it." and carefully studied the corpse making sure not to disturb anything. Took pictures and videos of everything in the lab, dusted the bone-handled knife, and everything for fingerprints. Ruthie noticed a slight bulge in Art's left suit coat pocket. Carefully removed it and said, "A golden bear stickpin. Is that yours, Cynthia?"

"No, I'm fond of cute and cuddly kittens, not smelly old bears."

Ruthie then inquired, "Does Ruth like bears?"

"I don't know I never bothered to ask her."

"Do you think we can go to her place and find out?" question Ruthie.

Close to 5:00 that afternoon, Cynthia knocked on the door of a beautiful blue Victorian house that set up on a hill. Ruth answered the door with a smile, glanced at George and Ruthie, and said, "Come on in, I'll put on a pot of tea."

As they sat in the parlor drinking tea, Ruthie took the bear stickpin out of her jean pocket and politely asked, "Ruth, do you like bears? I came across this one and I'm looking for someone to give it to."

Ruth quickly snatched the bear from Ruthie's hands, squealed with excitement saying, "My little Honey Bear, I thought I had lost this forever, wherever did you find it?"

"How do you know it's yours?"

"You see that little nick in the left ear. I did that when I dropped it, and on the back, there is the letter R, scratched on it, It's mine alright."

Ruthie took a sip of her tea and asked, "What happened between you and Art if you don't mind me asking."

"Art who?" questioned a nervous Ruth.

"Art Boulder. The guy that owned the farm with the lab underneath the barn."

"I never met him."

"He sure knows you," stated Ruthie, "Because he has a photo of you showing more than you should buy his cot in the lab."

"That picture can't be me," stated Ruth growing nervous.

Ruthie spotted a picture sitting on the fireplace mantel, walked to it, and picked it up, and inquired, "Is this a picture of Art Boulder standing next to you?"

Ruth marched to the fireplace, snatched the photo out of Ruthie's hand saying, "You're a nosey bugger aren't you."

Cynthia casually walked to Ruth, yanked the photo out of her hands, saying, "Why are you denying the fact that you know Art? Especially when you two were lover's way before I walked out on him for being lewd around me."

Ruth got in Ruthie's face and asked, "Are you trying to get me to say that I killed Art? Well, I didn't."

Ruthie smiled and said, "I never said anything about Art Boulder being murdered. The word on the street is that he is missing."

George approached Ruth and stated, "The two policemen that tried to falsely arrest my wife during the wedding reception said that a lady friend of Art reported him missing and went to his farm to search for evidence. The only lady friend Art had, was you. So, what did you do to Art? Oh, one other thing, right after Cynthia's money was stolen from the bank, you suddenly became rich. Care to explain?"

"You have just worn out your welcome. Now, please leave." Stated Ruth firmly.

Back at George's farm in 1891, Cynthia asked, "Why can't we just zip back to when Art was murdered and nab the killer in the act?"

George stated, "We can't do that because we don't know when Art was stabbed."

Ruthie walked into the farmhouse after George and his wife and questioned,

"Cynthia, why did you break up with Art?"

"He wanted me to do something that was immorally wrong. So, I called a halt to our courtship."

"Did you give Ruth, that, bear stick pin?"

"Yes, I did. My mother gave it to me and since I didn't like bears and my mother was gone home to be with the Lord, I gave it to Ruth."

"In other words, you gave Ruth the bear stick pin right after you stabbed Art to put the blame on her. She took the pin and dropped it nicking the left ear. You then picked it up and planted the pin on Art's dead body. Very clever."

"I gave her the pin long before Art was murdered."

"So, you say."

"Yes! I say so." screamed an aggravated Cynthia.

"What about Rubin? Have you seen him since he got fresh with you when he wanted you to cooked dinner for him that afternoon?"

"Rubin was crude, rude, and rough and always manhandled me every time he came to my cottage."

"You like being manhandled by Rubin."

George shouted, "That will be enough of your off the wall questioning Ruthie. My wife was pure when we married."

"I'm just going on what I found on the internet."

"Are you sure you were reading about the right Cynthia Atwater?"

"Duhhh!"

George turned to his wife and questioned, "What about Rubin?"

"He was a woodsman and manhandled me every time he came into my cottage which I hated. One afternoon, Rubin walked in the back door, took off his muddy shoes and shirt, and sat in the parlor smoking his pipe bare-chested, which embarrass me to no end. When I ask him what he wanted for dinner? He pulled me down on his lap and kiss me over and over again which terrified me because I thought he was going to do more than kiss me."

"How did you get rid of the guy?" questioned George.

"I told Pastor Tumwater after church one Sunday and he stood in the doorway that afternoon and would not allow Rubin to enter. Rubin tried to push the Pastor out of the way and he sent him flying on his butt."

"So, you and Rubin never mixed it up at any time?" questioned Ruthie.

"No, and don't ask me about Don Hollister either. He was a pain where I sit and I am glad he is out of my life for good."

"A little touchy aren't we."

Cynthia reframed herself from blowing her top at Ruthie and calmly inquired, "Do you want me to question you about your private life and why you did what you did with those guys?"

"No, but I'm not a murder suspect, you are."

George put his right arm around his wife's waist saying, "Ruthie, I hired you to find the one who killed Art, not badger Cynthia. If you can't do that, I can always open a Time Arch in your bedroom, then slide you and your bed through to Bangor, Maine in 1723."

"In other words, I do what you say or I am literally history," stated Ruthie smiling.

"Now you get the picture."

"It's hard for me to believe that your wife dated several men and never got in bed with them," stated Ruthie

Cynthia calmly explained, "In my time the men never went swimming with women. Our bathing suits covered the entire body, as did the nightwear and the clothes. This means we had a high moral standard, If, you don't believe me check the internet yourself when we get back."

Ruthie hung her head and said, "Cynthia, I admire you and your strength, I wish I could slip back in time and say no sex to those guys."

George gave a sorrowful Ruthie a friendly hug and said, "To go back and change your past would change who you are today. Learn from your mistakes, repent, and go on in Christ."

7

Trapped in the past

Some three weeks later, George was watching TV in the den and said. "Cynthia, that preacher is right because that is something that has been churning around my heart for weeks. Why is it that the people that do not know Christ are more faithful to do what they say than God's children. We are faithful to Christ however, a lot of Saints when they say they will do something they don't and become known as untrustworthy. If we're going to be faithful to Christ we should be faithful to the brother in Christ and everyone around us as well. If we say we are going to do something we should do it. in other words, we should be a person of our word. But sad to say a lot of Saints are not like Daniel who had an excellent spirit and there was no fault found in him. If he could do it without the Baptism of the Holy Spirit we who are filled with the Spirit should be able to do it even more so."

"Did Ruthie pull a no show again today?" questions Cynthia.

"Yes, and if she does it one more time, I will go back in time to the day we met her and change the timeline so we don't meet."

"Give Ruthie room to make mistakes, encourage her and relax we'll find the killer." Cynthia then silently stared at her husband wondering if he would do the same to her if he got mad at her. George saw the worried look on his wife's face. Had her sit with him on the couch, put his arm around her, kissed her then said, "I would never do that to you. Besides, I put an algorithm in the time computer so that It will skip over those days. In other words, the day that I met you and our wedding cannot be accessed through the Time Arch."

"So, you are not going to hold that over my head every time we have an argument!"

"Why would I do a thing like that when I love you,"

"You were ready to erase Ruthie when she begin to mess up. What would stop you from doing the same to me?"

"The conviction of the Spirit that's what."

Cynthia smiled devilishly and asked, "Can we go back in time and arrange it so I don't meet Ruth?"

George growled, "Cynthia. I am surprised at you for making an evil statement like that. Ruth was a good friend of yours."

"Friend?" questioned Cynthia. "Are you kidding? She was a backstabbing Weasel. She buttered me up so she could find where my money was and tell Art."

"Then tell me why is Art dead and Ruth is rich if she was working for him?"

"Somebody that knew me had to plant that stuff so it would look like I did it and it was not Art who set me up."

"Are you sure you gave Ruth the bear stick pin before Art, was murdered?"

"Yes, I am sure."

Ruthie walked in clad in jean hot pants and a skimpy blue halter top with her nose stuck in an old notebook. Sat on the couch with George and said, "I found part of Art's journal and the last few paged tells about him and Cynthia."

Cynthia cleared her throat and said, "Did you forget that I am right here?"

Ruthie smiled and said, "Oh hi C. didn't see you there. I've dug up more evidence that proved that you killed Art in a jealous rage. See what Art wrote on August 29th, 1885. I was afraid that Cynthia was going to stab me with the bone-handled knife because she flew into a rage when she found out that I had tea with Ruth White. Ruthie then stated, "This is proof that you killed Art."

Cynthia studied the journal and said, "That isn't Art's handwriting. It's a poor forgery and I dumped Art on August 15th that year."

"So, you say."

Cynthia inquired politely, "Ruthie, what have you been doing this past 3 weeks?"

"I would walk in your home, have breakfast with George and we would go to the time lab and worked on the murder case."

"All total, how long have you known George and me?"

"About 4 weeks."

"Of which you spent most of them with my husband."

"Yeah, so what."

"In other words, you and my husband are buddy buddies."

Ruthie snickered and stated, "You should have been in the lab when Georgie," Ruthie paused mid-sentence and stated, "I'll meet you in the time lab, Georgie."

Cynthia bellowed, "Ruthie Susan White! Don't take another step. Now, turn around and listen to what I have to say! One, you will not walk into my home without knocking anymore! You will address George as Sir, and me as Ma'am! You will not work with George alone anymore. We are paying you top dollar to find Art Boulder's killer and not find a reason to get me out of the way so you can step in! Is that clear Miss. White? Furthermore, when you come to work wearing skimpy clothes, you will put on a lab coat and button it. is that clear? And the next time I catch you walking around the time lab in your underwear, I will personally open a portal over a volcano in shove you in, now put on a lab coat and get to work!"

"So, sue me, I was hot, alright!"

"I don't care how hot you were, you are to wear modest attire around my husband at all times."

Yes, ma'am." Stated Ruthie sarcastically

"Oh, your break is at ten-thirty and will last for 15 minutes and your lunch will start at twelve and will last for one-half hour. I will have these rules typed up for you to sign at lunch time. You are dismissed, Miss. White."

George stared at his wife with his mouth open in shock then stated, "I have never seen you so worked up."

"There have been many marriages that went south because the husband or wife was way too friendly with the partner's friend." Cynthia stared into George's eyes saying, "You're mine, and I will claw the eyes out of anyone who tried to take you away from me. Now, what happened in the lab that Ruthie was talking about? Or do I really want to know?"

"It was no big deal."

"Then you won't mind telling me."

"I got up from my desk, spun around, bumped into Ruthie and fell on top of her. No big deal."

"If it is no big deal then why are you sweating?"

"Well, I ah."

"I'm just playing with you Babe. Let's see what Ruthie is up to."

"In the time lab, George hollered, "Ruthie, where did you go?"

Cynthia picked up a note on George's desk that said, "Went back in time to do some investigating. She showed it to George who said, "That idiot. I told her hundreds of times not to use the Time Arch alone."

"Don't worry. She can get back when she wants,"

"Ruthie doesn't have her Arch Retrieval Communicator because it is right here on the desk. So, she is stuck in the past, until we go fetch her."

"I've never seen you use an Arch Retrieval Communicator before."

George took out a small silver flip cell phone and said, "It is something new and is why I carry this old cell phone along with my Smartphone. It's the Arch Retrieval Communicator and I carry a backup in the heal of my shoe. Sweet, put this mother of pearl necklace on you. It's your Arch Retrieval Communicator. Don't lose it."

George checked the time location and said, "Ruthie went to 1885. I bet she is going to question Art."

"That's not good," stated Cynthia. "Because Art has a short fuse when people fire all kinds of questions at him."

George set the Time Arch for August 1st 5 PM 1885 so Art would not be there, Entered with his wife then checked the lab under the barn. George asked, "Cynthia Sweet. You know Art's lab better than I do. Does it look like Ruthie has been here?"

Cynthia slowly inhaled then stated, "She was here because I can smell her heavy scented hand lotion. But Art's lab looks normal. Wait a minute. The blanket on the cot should not be draped that low."

George lifted the blanket and saw Ruthie stuffed under the cot, bound hand, and foot. Hauled Ruthie out from under the cot, untied her, and gave her something to wipe the blood from her lip then asked, "What's the big idea using the time Arch when I told you not to."

"Sorry Sir, it won't happen again."

"It better not because the next time we may not be able to find you. Here is your Arch Retrieval Communicator. Go back to the lab, make out a report about what happened between you and Art and put something on besides those hot pants and that halter top."

"Do you want me to put down the personal stuff That went on during my trips into the past' Sir?"

"Yes, that stuff yes."

"But Sir, I don't want what I did with Art to be public news."

"As a Christian, you should not be doing something immoral, because you will have no job."

"When I said personal, I meant what he said to me and so on."

"If Art threatened you in any way Ruthie, I need to know."

"Yes, Sir. But when Ruthie couldn't open a time Arch to return to her own time. George explained, "I was afraid this would happen. Your Time Arch Retrieval Communicator wasn't with you when you enter the arch so it could record the mild magnetic signature that the arch puts on your body."

"In other words, nobody from the past can snoop around in the future, which means I am stuck in the past." moaned Ruthie.

"Exactly," stated George.

"That's just great, Say hi to my great-great grandkids for me."

"I can always come back when I bought the farm in 1890 then I could open an arch back to your time."

"Unacceptable," growled Ruthie, "You need to come up with another way besides leaving me stranded here in the past."

"How about if I just forget that you exist altogether."

"No, no, no, no, no, not acceptable!" stated a panicky Ruthie.

Cynthia hit George in his side saying, "Will you stop giving Ruthie a hard time."

"I'm only kidding. Don't worry Ruthie we'll stay with you until we can figure this dilemma out. But first, we should get out of Art's lab before he catches us."

Cynthia stated, "What if we arrange it so we don't meet Ruthie, then run into her later and hire her. That would put her back in the normal time."

George glanced at Ruthie and said, "Knowing her, she would pull the same dumb stunt and put us in the same predicament." George gazed at his wife and inquired, "Where does Rubin live?"

"We need to get out of this lab before we are caught by Art."

Sitting in a park some miles away, Ruthie stated, "Here is my report on Art. I exited the arch behind a haystack, walked up to Art as he was entering the barn and asked him what he knew about Ruth. He inquired, "Why do you want to know"

"Are you involved with her romantically?" I asked.

Art brought me into his lab, then asked me who I really was. When I would not tell him, he belted me and shouted, "You're a reporter aren't you!" picked up the bone-handled knife to stab me when Ruth hollered from the other side of the lab door, "Hey Sugar! I have news concerning Cynthia!"

The next thing I remember is you hauling me out from under the cot."

"Is there anything else you can tell me?"

"Yeah. Art has an 8-inch scar on his back just below his left shoulder."

Cynthia stated, "That proves that Ruth was playing around with Art while he was courting me and the bone-handled knife belongs to him."

George questioned his wife, "How did you know Art had a scar on his back?"

"No. I never saw him with his shirt off and he never divulge how he got it. But, if you two will behave yourselves, I'll find Ruth, question her and find out." Cynthia gave George a kiss and left.

Twenty-three minutes later, Cynthia approached Ruth from behind, clad in a long black dress and said, "Hey Knock Knees. What are you doing here?"

"Cyn, nice seeing you out of your cottage for a change."

"You want to talk over a cup of tea?"

Sitting at a table in a diner, Cynthia took a sip of her hot lemon, tea and inquired, "Court any interesting men lately?"

"There is this one cute guy I have been seeing who is an inventor and owns a farm. The other day I visited him while he was chopping wood with his shirt off and I just had to ask him how he got the scar on his back."

"Oh, how? Was he in a fight?" question Cynthia.

"Don't tell anyone but he was robbing a bank when a bank guard slashed him with a knife, which caused him to drop the money. Fortunately, he got away and they could not identify the robber. Of course, you know me, I made him breakfast When I got up the next morning."

"Why on Earth would you court a crook and commit an immoral act with him?"

"Because he's my kind of a man if you know what I mean,"

"In other words, he takes what he wants and doesn't care who gets in his way."

Ruth hung her head and said, "I know that it is wrong to fool around with a man when I am not married but I don't have the strength to say no the way you do."

"Ruth, you're just like me when I was single. But I didn't go down the path you did because the Lord gave me strength through the finished work on the Cross. I said no to fornication because of what Christ did and not what I could do."

"One of these days I'll give my life to Christ but not today. Sorry. It's been nice talking to you but I have to meet Art and can't be late or he will blow his top."

A short time later, Cynthia greeted her husband and reported, "Art was stabbed in the back by a guard when he tried to rob a bank last year. He also has a bad temper and Ruth is heavily involved with Art but is petrified to leave him."

Ruthie questioned, "Not to get off the subject but what is your computer experience?"

"Are you concerned that I may be a hack?" question George.

"You know."

George then explained, "Ok here goes. My first computer was a Tandy HX1000 which I bought at Radio Shack in 1993. I then upgraded to windows 3.1 that was powered by DOS 2.0, and I still have that five and a quarter floppy. I have had very little problems with the computers I have owned. A couple of years ago, I contacted a technician who got into my computer via the Internet to fix the problem. He restored my computer to a good running condition. However, he botched up the communication between the computer and the printer and I had to call him back to fix it. While trying to fix the problem he crashed the operating system. He called me back and said that I needed a Windows upgrade which I refused because of a lack of income, and he disconnected from my computer. However, my wallpaper did not return and left me with a black computer screen. I finally restored the wallpaper to my computer, but there was still something wrong and I had to call the tech back to get the situation straightened out. From then on, I studied the ins and outs of computers and invented the HJO Capacitor which powers the magnetic field around the Time Arch interrupting the delicate balance between the past and future allowing me to easily slip through time."

Ruthie stared at George with her mouth opened then said, "Yeah. In English please."

"Do you know what a portal is?"

"Yeah, it's a two-dimensional gateway between two points."

"The Time Arch is a two-dimensional gateway through time."

"And my Time Arch Retrieval Communicator keeps me linked to my time by recording the magnetic signature. I'm dead without that signature on my Retrieval Communicator."

Cynthia stated, "Have faith. There is an answer to this predicament we just have to find it that's all."

8

Ruthie's back

Hours later, George, Cynthia, and Ruthie sat at a round, rod iron table with a glass top at a sidewalk café in Knoxville. Cynthia stared at two men standing across the street from them and stated, "That's Art over there talking to Pete Wilburn, a well-known Thug and drug dealer."

George sighed, then stated, "This murder case concerning Art's death just became complicated." George then saw the Cynthia of 1885, approach Pete, shake his hand. He gave her a 12-inch square package neatly tied up in brown paper, then handed her a fat white envelope. George turned to his wife and asked, "Do you want to tell me why you are a courier for a drug lord?"

"Did you forget that in June of 1890 I was murdered but you saved my life so I didn't kill Art."

"Don't forget that once I save you from being brutally slashed to death by that killer, the timeline changed. This means the shame and embarrassment of Art trying to seduce you in his lab tormented you, so you used my Time Arch to seek revenge. Now explain to me why you were delivering drugs for a known drug dealer while you were dating Art?"

"Pete told me that it was medical supplies and I didn't know he was a drug dealer until after I refused to deliver any more packages for him."

"That's probably why someone tried to kill you. Pete figured that you knew too much and was going to squeal to the police and hired someone to take you out. But explain to me why there are several places where someone used my Time Arch and tried to erase the log entry on the computer? Don't blame it on Ruthie because this was before we were married."

Feeling trapped, Cynthia stated, "I, ah, had to go back in time to my place and take care of a few things to prepare for the wedding and I didn't know I erased the computer entries."

Ruthie took a swallow of her coffee then stated, "George Sir. I did some checking and found out that Art was reported missing in late October of 1885. This means you Cynthia was dating Art just before he was reported missing."

Cynthia gazed at her husband and Ruthie and questioned, "Hey. What is this? Let's gang up on Cynthia day? I know what's going on. Ruthie, you are still trying to get rid of me so you can have George. But, it will not work. He's my husband and I'll do everything in my power to stop you. Yes, Art Boulder was reported missing because he took a trip to Virginia for some unknown reason and never told anybody."

"It is not my fault that all the evidence leads to you as the killer," stated Ruthie in defense. "And I am not out to get your husband."

"Then why is it that every time you come to the house to work on the case. You walk right by me as if I'm not there and talk to George for over thirty minutes before going to work?"

"I told you that I am not stalking your husband; you are just letting your imagination run away with you."

"You think so. It's not my imagination that I have to stand outside of the bedroom door in the mornings to keep you out when my husband is dressing."

"Can we change the subject to something else?" stated Ruthie.

"What's the matter Ruthie, uneasy because I'm getting too close to the truth."

Ruthie reached in her leather satchel, took out Art's journal, turned to June 7, 1885, and stated, "This is only part of art Journal where the rest is I don't know. But he wrote in his journal that after he met you that sunny afternoon in June, he took you to his lab and you two spent the rest of the day on his cot. But I don't have to tell you because you already know what you two did. So, don't play the oh so innocent with me Cynthia. Because I know that you are using George to cover up your who you really are."

An angry Cynthia stated, "I don't know where you got that so-called Journal from but that's not how it happened and I don't have a sorted past you Cheap Hussy."

Ruthie stood, got in Cynthia's face, and stated through clenched teeth, "You call me that again and you will be spitting out your teeth."

Cynthia sprang to her feet and landed a hard right cross to Ruthie's jaw. Her eyes rolled back in her head and she collapsed on the sidewalk out cold.

Cynthia then held her hand saying, "Ow, ow, ow, ow. I think I broke my hand on her jaw."

George went to check his wife's hand but she pushed him away saying, "Get away from me."

"If you're mad at me because of what I said about you, I'm sorry but all the evidence still points to you as Art's killer."

"I forgive you, but I think we should pick Ruthie up off the sidewalk before somebody thinks that she's drunk."

George placed his hands underneath Ruthie's armpits to put her on a black rod iron chair. Her white button down blouse, slipped out of her jeans to expose a 6 inch diameter bruise on her stomach and stated, "I don't think Ruthie was telling us the truth about what happened with her and Art."

Still unconscious, George sat Ruthie in the chair, Cynthia had two ladies hold up a red and white checkered tablecloth for some privacy. She open Ruthie's blouse and found several nasty burns on her side and stated, "Someone tortured her. Most likely it was Art."

Ruthie opened her eyes, and shouted, "Hey what do you think you're doing?" and quickly closed her Top.

Cynthia rose to her feet and stated forcefully, "What really happened between you an arc in his lab and no more fabrications this time, I want the truth."

"I exited the time arch and met Art outside the barn and began to ask him some questions. He brought me into his lab under the barn and knocked me out. When I came too, I was lying on his cot with my hands and feet tide and he was holding a hot iron in his hand. When I wouldn't tell him what he wanted to know he burned my side. So, I told him that I was from the future and we were investigating his murder. Whether or not he believed me I don't know and what we did after that it's none of your business."

With Ruthie's burns taken care of, she quickly glanced around and questioned, "Where is Art's journal?"

Cynthia smiled then stated, "The waitress took it when she cleaned our table."

"I need that journal for evidence in the case." cried Ruthie.

"You just want it, so you can throw more garbage at me that isn't true?"

"I haven't begun to expose you for what you are."

"And what is that pray tell?"

"Aright, you asked for it. Art told me that you are hooked on the drug Laudanum and have several bottles stashed somewhere."

"I have a bottle of that nasty stuff because I had a bad cold."

"Admit it, you are hooked on the stuff and are hiding it from hubby."

George saw that his wife was ready to fall apart emotionally from Ruthie's ruthless bombardment of insults. Took his Arch Communicator out of his pocket and tapped in a code.

A puzzled Ruthie inquired, "What are you doing?"

"I'm entering an access code to override your Arch Communicator so I can send you back to your time. Because I need you to dig up all the information on a Don Hollister that you can. He may be a key to this murder case. George kissed Ruthie on the side of her face, tapped enter, then pushed her. Ruthie fell backward through the table and landed in her own time.

Cynthia threw her arms around her husband, gave him a long passionate kiss on his lips, then stated, "The thorn in my side is finally gone. Yes, yes, yes!"

"Let's have another cup of coffee and two bowels of Steamed Walnut Pudding with caramel sauce. Then you can tell me about why is Ruth trying to destroy your good name?"

"I have had a weak friendship with Ruth ever since we were in our early teens. Of course, we were boy crazy back then. Ruth wanted to take off on a weekend with a boy she just met. I told her father and he grounded her for a month. From then on she has had it in for me."

"Why did you squeal on her?"

"Because he was into gamboling bigtime and I was scared that Ruth would wind up in jail. Which he did."

George thought for a moment then stated, "Do you supposed Ruth told her bitterness about you to her children and grandchildren and is the reason why Ruthie is bent on destroying you?"

"And Possibly the reason why she stole my money."

"Hey, if we hurry, we can make it to the bank in time to close your account and prevent Ruth from stealing your money,"

"No. Let her have the money. I have the Lord, the Love of my Life, and a stash of cash in the bank so I am good. A woman by the name of Maria is holding a tent meeting in a field, not a mile from here. You want to go?"

"Sure, why not."

After the tent meeting, George was explaining to a man how Christ provided everything for him through His death on the Cross. A shabby dressed young woman caught Cynthia's attention and told her that her little boy needs attention and could she help. Cynthia followed the woman behind the tent, quickly glanced around and questioned, "Hey, what's going on?"

The woman smiled and said, "Meet my boyfriend."

A hand firmly grabbed Cynthia's right shoulder and spun her around, and she stared at a middle-aged man dressed in buckskin. He waved a hunting knife in her face and said, "Hand over your money or I'll bury this blade in you."

"No. because all I have to do is scream and this place will be swarming with people."

As the man raised his knife to plunge it in Cynthia's chest. His complexion suddenly turned pale, dropped his knife, and tore off through the field screaming in terror.

Cynthia caught the gentle fragrance of roses, smiled and whispered, "Thank you, Father, for protecting me. It is true that You, Lord Jesus guard Your own."

Cynthia walked back to where her husband was, who had just finished praying for an elderly man. George took his wife's hand, walked up the street and rented a room at a motel for the night. He sat on the edge of the bed with its squeaky springs and inquired, "Cynthia, I am having a problem praying for people. That old gentleman I was praying for when you walked up, nothing happens after I prayed for him. Did I do something wrong?"

"No, you didn't. You are just a conduit for the power of the Spirit to flow through. Remember this, you minister in the power of the Holy Spirit then leave the results to God. However, you also need to cultivate a relationship with the Saviour by reading, praying, above all learn to have a worshipful thankful heart. By doing that, the Father will respond by drawing close to you and show you where you have to straighten up in your walk with Him."

The next morning, George sat on the edge of the bed and moaned, "This mattress didn't do my back any good."

"Lay on your stomach Babe and I'll fix that in a jiffy."

Lying on his stomach on the bed with Cynthia sitting on his hips. George let go a scream and hollered, "Take it easy on my back will ya! I want to be able to walk after my back rub."

"My dad's sister showed me how to loosen up a person's back by doing it to me."

"In other words, I'm your first victim."

"You could say that," stated Cynthia snickering. Hey, I think it's time we dressed and had breakfast because I want to question Rubin today."

Just as George had finished buttoning his short-sleeved shirt, a Time Arch appeared close to Cynthia and Ruthie boldly exited it shouting, "I am back for more fun."

Cynthia grumbled, "Go play in a buffalo stampede will ya."

"Is that any way to talk to your best bud?" stated Ruthie.

George stood between Cynthia and Ruthie saying, "Go downstairs and reserve a table for us. My wife and I will be there in a bit."

After Ruthie had left, Cynthia questioned, "Sweet, is there a way you can open a time vortex right under her?"

"Be nice."

"How do you be nice to a woman that's trying to take you away from me?"

"Ruthie is just being friendly that's all."

"I see the way she looks at you, and no I am not imagining things because a woman knows when there is someone after her mate."

9

Lauren's testimony

Later, Cynthia, George, and Ruthie sat at a square oak table in the hotel dining room. Cynthia ordered eggs over easy, sausage, and grits. George ordered steak and eggs while Ruthie ordered a mushroom omelet with home fries and toast. George wrote on a slip of paper, 062418901000 A Beta. Gave it to his wife saying, "I need you to type this in your Arch Communicator when you get the chance."

Cynthia quickly glanced around the room, saw that it was empty, took her Communicator and fumbled around trying to enter the code. Ruthie took the communicator from Cynthia, entered the code in seconds then handed it back. Cynthia took the communicator saying, "Ruthie, could you be a dear and get my purse from our room?"

After Ruthie left, Cynthia stated, "Did you notice Ruthie's hair is a lot longer than when she left, and for someone who is a greenhorn around time computers, she is quite skillful with the Arch Communicator. I think she has been using the Time Arch behind your back and has been talking to Ruth about me."

"Forgive me for accusing you of you using the arch behind my back because I saw how inept you were trying to enter that code and how nimble Ruthie was."

Cynthia stated, "What I am saying is when you sent Ruthie to do some research in the lab, she spent months learning how to use your Time Arch. How else did her hair grow that long so fast? I have just one question. You are in the Time Lab and set the Time Arch for your destination and walk through the arch without an Arch Communicator. How would you get back?"

"The Arch would detect that I didn't have my communicator and erect a mild force field to prevent me from entering."

"Then tell me how Ruthie was able to use the Arch without her Arch Communicator?"

George placed his hands on his head saying, "I'm so stupid. She was using me so she could use my Time Arch for her own purpose."

"Which means we have to find out why Ruthie is trying to get rid of me by pinning the murder on me? So, the next time she bats those fake eyelashes at you, ignore her."

"What do you say we go back to our time and check out Ruthie's place?"

"I thought you'd never ask."

George entered a time code in his Arch Communicator so it would open in Ruthie's home in 2020.

Cynthia ordered, "Babe, you check the den and I'll check her bedroom."

In the den, George knelt in front of a metal filing cabinet, opened it, and found file after fie of people's ancestors. He then studied Ruthie's notebook and realized that she had a thriving business of researching people's family trees and a time machine would be just the thing to put her on Easy Street.

Cynthia tapped her husband on his right shoulder, showed him an old photo and asked, "Recognize the women in this picture?"

"That's you and Ruth standing on the steps of the church."

"That means Ruthie knew we were into time travel when she saw us in Starbucks because she recognized me from this photo. What did you find?"

"Ruthie has a thriving business researching people's family trees."

Cynthia opened the filing cabinet, leafed through the folders until she came to the one that was labeled Ruth. Opened it and found a dozen pictures of Cynthia and two hundred typed written pages on her saying how unfair Cynthia treated her great-great-great-grandmother. Cynthia shoved the folder back in the filing cabinet screaming, "Ruthie, I am gonna strangle you when I see you!"

George put his arm on his wife's shoulder saying, "Right now you need to let it go before you give yourself a heart attack."

An enraged Cynthia hollered, "Did you see what Ruthie wrote about me? She called me a Tramp and a liar and I destroyed her relationship with Art and she took the money from me that I stole from her! So, help me I'm gonna kill her!"

George smiled and inquired. "Do you want to get back at Ruthie? Let's see what she has in her refrigerator that we can devour."

In Ruthie's kitchen, Cynthia opened the refrigerator door and said, "Babe, you grab the half cheesecake and I'll take the Coke."

Back at George's farm, they pigged out on the cheesecake and Coke. He looked at his wife and stated, "What if I create an algorithm that would only allow certain DNA through the time Arch?"

"Knowing Ruthie, she would probably get ticked off and destroy the arch. However, could you design something that will keep track of who uses the time arch and where they go? But, the individual shouldn't know that they are being tracked."

"I can write an algorithm that will ask for a password,"

Cynthia asked, "What about a Backup Tracker that will scan who used the arch, where they go, and the time they enter the arch? But, make it so only you and I will have access to it. This way when Ruthie uses the arch we will know where, when and who."

"That is a great idea, give me a day or two to set it up."

"I feel funny leaving Ruthie stranded in the past."

"All we have to do is set the Time Arch a few minutes after we left, and make sure that we are dressed the way we left,"

A week later, George finished installing the Backup Tracker, set the Time Arch for thirty seconds after they left and had just sat down when Ruthie walked up to Cynthia with her purse.

George stated, "It's time we got to work and set his Arch Communicator for 062518901100-A and entered the Arch with Ruthie and his wife.

A few miles north of Rockford, Tennessee the three stepped out of the arch and George inquired, "Cynthia, where does Rubin live from here?"

"I am not sure. I have never been to his cabin."

Ruthie pointed to a narrow path that passed a large boulder on the left and said, "I've done my homework and he lived 2 and a half miles up that path."

At Rubin's cabin, he was on the right side of the log cabin splitting wood without his shirt. He stopped, stared at Cynthia, and growled, "I see you have someone new to give me a hard time."

"If you would have minded your manners in my home, I would not have to have the Pastor throw you out of my house."

"What did I do that was so bad?"

"I rather not talk about it. Oh, this is my husband, George, and my friend Ruthie."

Rubin stared at her and commented, "She looks a lot like a young Ruth if you ask me."

George asked, "What do you know about Art?"

"You mean the one who use to own the farm? Nothing. But I hear that he is missing and I hope he stays that way."

"How did you feel when Art dated Cynthia and not you?"

"She can court whoever she likes."

"You were maneuvering yourself into position so you could get cozy with Cynthia, along comes Art, and you are out in the cold. Now you are telling me that you didn't care about her."

"Yup. Now get lost,"

"If you don't have any feelings for Cynthia, then why did you try to kiss her when you were in her parlor, shirtless?"

Rubin quickly spun around, belted George on his chin and said, "That's my business, now get off my land!"

Cynthia glanced at Ruthie then at her husband then stated, "We'd better be going."

George stated, "Cynthia, I'm not finished questioning him." Gazed at Rubin and said, "Art is missing and you have an attitude which tells me that you know something."

Rubin took a swing with his ax and almost buried the blade in the chopping block, stared at George and stated, "Yeah, I have a problem with that worthless piece of garbage! Because of him, my cozen Wilma has to spend the rest of her life in a wheelchair."

"Oh? Why is that?"

"Wilma was visiting Art and was at the top of the stairs when he started an argument with her, pushed her down the stairs and broke her back. He claims that she slipped and fell but, I believe Wilma When she told me that Art pushed her."

"It sounds like a case of he said, she said."

"Cynthia knows too well that Art has a bad temper and is a tyrant."

George stared at his wife and inquired, "Did Art ever hit you?"

Cynthia gazed at the ground and stated, "I am sorry that I didn't tell you, Babe. Art hit me across my face with the back of his hand several times because I did something that he disapproved of."

Rubin asked, "Cyn, why don't you tell your husband what you told me concerning Art"

Cynthia explained, "It was three months into courting Art when he barged into my house early in the morning screaming and shouting and accusing me of stealing his invention. When I told him that I didn't, he hit me in my stomach and called me a liar as I doubled over in pain, He grabbed my hair and pulled my head back and smashed my face into the kitchen wall. Rubin came in, saw what Art was doing to me and beat the snot out of him."

Rubin stated, "I tended to Cynthia's wounds that week and told her not to go back with him when he comes begging."

Ruthie asked, "Cynthia, is that why you stabbed Art in the chest?"

Silence ruled for a minute then Rubin stated, "Cynthia doesn't have the heart to kill so if Art is dead it wasn't Cyn."

George glanced at his wife as she picked up something from the ground. Then said to Rubin, "Don't go anywhere, I might want to ask you a few more questions."

Back at George's farm in 2020, he opened an arch to Ruthie's bedroom a minute in the future and gave her a hug before she entered. Cynthia made a pot of herbal tea and served it to her husband in the parlor. Then asked, "What did you find on the ground when I was asking Rubin questions?"

"Ruthie's smartphone."

"What do you say that we put time travel aside for a while and go to the mall and hang out at Starbucks?"

Cynthia shouted, "The last one to the car buys the coffee."

At Starbucks in the mall, A woman in her fifties clad in a pink and white, broad vertical striped short sleeve shirt and jeans wheeled up to their table and greeted, "George. What are you up to these days? Mr. B. and I haven't seen you in a long time."

"I've been traveling a lot, Oh, Lauren, this is my wife Cynthia."

"Far out, you got married,"

Cynthia inquired, "Lauren, do you mind me asking you why you're in a wheelchair?"

"I had headaches for as long as I can remember but those were different, I settled with Buffern, but it wasn't helping then I switched to Excedrin which was supposed to be better. The headaches or migraines became more and more impossible to live with. It wasn't my fault; I just had the headaches along with the migraines and my lack of physical coordination was noticed by my Godparents in Maine.

Cynthia inquired, "Were you living on your own at that time?"

"Yes, which was very difficult, so I rode the brain cancer bridal for as long as I could. My stepmother got up early every morning for 6 weeks to make me breakfast. Which she served me fried eggs with toast or my favorite pancakes. She wanted to make sure that I had food in my tummy and didn't know that I would put on pounds. Everyone knows that a patient shouldn't gain weight.

At the New Haven Hospital, I went through 6 weeks of radiation therapy, which was where I learned. If someone tells you to stay still so I can get this right you stay still! I didn't want to because I didn't want all that radiation in my head. But the gospel according to my surgent, I wouldn't get any better. That's when I was put in the Connecticut Hospice in Branford because I looked like death itself and my skin was blue, in other words, I was dying."

"Did you know the Lord at that time?" question, Cynthia.

"Yes, and Christ gave me His peace all through the ordeal. Anyways, at the Hospice, I got anything I wanted to eat, and I could do anything I wanted within reason. The guy I was going with at the time Mike Clancy used to take me for walks around the Hospice. I went home on the weekends and still possess the ability to walk only now I had to walk holding onto someone or something. One of the doctors at the Hospice taught me something that has come in handy: it was not to do anything foolish, irresponsible, or dangerous or FID for short. His name was Doctor Brenner. I'm sure he be very surprised if I were to go back to that Hospice. Besides all the pluses of the hospice, there were chosen minutes for me to deal with, for instance, There were at least 6 women with me on that Ward. At night we would go to bed not knowing who wouldn't wake up in the morning. More often than enough one or two didn't make it through the night."

"Did it bother you that some of your roommates died during the night?" asked Cynthia.

"You better believe it did. I had a hard time going to sleep every night because I would worry if I would be next.

On the rare occasion that I was invited to go back to Hamden, to my dad's house, I used to play backgammon with my older sister. Because of the chemotherapy and radiation that I had to endure I had gained a lot of weight, 140 to 165 pounds. Well anyway, I used to play backgammon. My sister would roll the dice and got a good role she would, holler, "Big moose, big moose because I had gained so much weight. All that proves is that I was fed up with her constantly making fun of me that I called her on it. So, I told her to stop making fun of me, that I couldn't help to be the way I was. My sister explained that she wasn't calling me "a big Moose!" she was just saying Big Boost when she got a good roll on the dice.

At about that time my dad explained to me that since I had terminal brain cancer he had taken the liberty to buy me a Cemetery plot. It was situated right next to where my mother was buried at All Saints Cemetery in North Haven, Connecticut. This was actually more than I could take. I took a deep breath, believed in God for his best, and said, "Dad, I'm not going to use that plot, why? Because you are going to use it first." Less than a year later he died.

My mother had died of breast, bone and then brain cancer when I was 11. So, you see I had my mother for 11 years and my father for 22 years. After, Pastor Champlin and a few saints from his church prayed for me. Right after they prayed for me, there was an immediate change and I looked like a healthy young woman again. I was transferred to New Britain Memorial Hospital in New Britain in April of 1984. Which does not exist anymore but is now called "The Hospital for Special Care" on Corbin Avenue in New Britain.

Back in 1984 when my father died I had been attending church a Cheshire. There I met Mr. B. who was in charge of picking up the Saints to bring to church. I was one of those who he transported to church so I could fellowship with God, Those trips to church soon became trips to McDonald's for a cup of tea, then perhaps, we went to Walnut Hill Park in New Britain. I had met the man that I knew God wanted me to marry. Now I know he was the one I was supposed to marry. However, The Lord in His infinite wisdom left me with hemiparesis, hydrocephalus, Psoriasis, and psoriatic arthritis. Because of the radiation I can hardly hear out of one ear, I have triple sometimes quadruple vision, my speech is slurred because of the medication I take to prevent me from having seizures. I have to use a wheelchair to get around because the radiation-damaged my inner ear which means I have a balance problem. Since I'm married Mister B. I have had kidney failure, skin cancer, breast cancer, and a bilateral mastectomy, liver problems, stomach problems, three brain operations and 2 shunts in my head. I also suffer from nightmares because of some things in the past. However, it ain't forever."

"Whoa! That's a powerful testimony," stated, Cynthia.

Lauren hung her head and said, "Last week Mister B. and I was at the kitchen stove making American Goulash for dinner. I looked at him and told him that I wanted a divorce because he needed a wife that could wash the clothes, clean the house, and take care of him, and not some cripple in a wheelchair." Lauren stared at Cynthia with tears running down her cheeks and stated, "Mister B. took me in his arms and told me how much he loved me. I truly have the man of my dreams. Hey, gotta go meet Mister B. Because he's gonna take me out for a steak dinner. Oh, the next time you're back in Connecticut drop by Bristol and pay us a visit."

Cynthia stated, "Here is our address, drop by and pay us a visit before you go back to Connecticut."

10

Cynthia strikes back

In the Time Lab under George's barn, he plugged Ruthie's smartphone into his computer and downloaded all her photos and text files. He then accessed the pictures and Cynthia stated, "This is where I take over." Sat in the chair behind the desk and leafed through the photos. The first picture was of Rubin splitting wood with no shirt on, the next five photos were of Ruth in her kitchen cooking, and one of George in the time lab without his shirt. Cynthia growled, "Do you want to explain to me why you had your shirt off?"

Ruthie spilled her hot coffee on me and I had to take off my shirt to prevent from being burned."

"Knowing Ruthie, she probably spilled the coffee on you to get you to remove it."

"Do I detect a note of jealousy?"

"I said this before, and I'll say it again, a woman knows when there is someone after her man."

Cynthia accessed an audio file named, 'The Real Truth' and heard Ruth say, "Sure I know Cynthia, we were close friends while we were growing up. If it weren't for me, Cynthia would be in jail because she walked up to a policeman one night while he was on duty and planted a long, wet kiss on his lips. I told the officer that she was drunk and fortunately, he believed me."

Ruthie questioned, "I heard that you stole Cynthia's money."

"Matter a fact it's the other way around, she conned my dad out of all his hard-earned money. All I did was get it back. So, who's the thief?"

"What do you think happened to Art?"

"He was an inventor and had a Lab under the barn. One day late in June, he told me that Cynthia wanted him to sleep with her that night. When Art refused, she went to his lab and screamed at him for over a half-hour then stabbed him with the bone-handled hunting knife that her father gave her."

Ruthie inquired, "Where were you when all this was happening?"

"I was just about to open the door to enter Art's lab when I heard Cynthia hollering at him. I quickly hid in the underground passageway that goes to the house from the barn and waited for her to leave. Then I went back to the lab and saw him lying on the floor with a knife in his chest. I would have called the police and reported it but I was scared to death that Cynthia was going to blame me for the murder. So, I closed Art's lab and left without telling anybody."

"In your opinion, is Cynthia a woman with high morals?"

"All I will say is, she has a red light on her front porch that she turns on for her male visitors in the evening."

Cynthia slammed her fist on the desk and screamed, "None of that is true!"

George tried to calm his wife down by saying, "Sweet, the Word says to cast all your care upon Christ for He cares for you. I know you want to strangle her but don't grieve the Holy Spirit with your anger."

"Don't preach to me about what I should do!"

"When was the last time you read the Bible?"

"Close to 2 weeks ago."

"Need I say more?"

"I'm sorry Babe, You are right, I got too involved with time travel and trying to figure out who murdered Art. Why don't you finish leafing through Ruthie's photos and I'll set by the time arch and read the Bible."

George stretched his arms towards his wife saying, "Give me a hug." Gave Cynthia a long-needed squeeze then sat at his desk, leafed through Ruthie's photos, and found a picture of a beautiful sunrise outside of Rubin's cabin, and questioned Ruthie's morals.

George accessed a text file called, 'Ruthie's Journal' and read, After my car accident, I was transported to the hospital where they put me on a stretcher by the nurse's station for I don't know how long. Then a doctor came up to me and stated, "You've been here for 20 hours and have waited long enough, so we are going to discharge you." I stated, "Sir, I live fifty miles from here and have a broken neck with no way to get home." He stated, "Find a ride because we are discharging you." He came back 20 minutes later with the same stern demeanor and asked, "Have you found a ride, yet?" I told him, "Yes, but she will be here tomorrow morning around 9. The doctor then stated, "We will dismiss you and you'll have to sit in the emergency waiting room until then." and left. I prayed and asked the Lord to change the doctor's mind so I could stay, The doctor came back 10 minutes later with a smile on his face and said, "OK compromise. We'll put you in one of the holding rooms.

George scrolled down several pages and read. I can sit in a chair with a Johnny coat and my shoes on and my neck brace on. The nurse told me that my balance isn't good. My friend Pearl brought two fat subs and coffee today which was a lot better than the hospital food that I have been eating. We talked about her boyfriend and how he is preparing to take his exam to be a pilot.

George scrolled down a few more pages and read, Home from the hospital and here I set in my deep blue recliner wishing for somebody to fix me some dinner and help me wash up. But, everyone is too busy to give me a hand.

Dick stopped by today, fixed dinner for me that will last a few days. He then was eager to help me in the shower, but I told him, no because he was too eager and I didn't like the smile on his face which told me that he was only interested in one thing and that was seeing my bare butt. So, I was determined not to give him a look-see.

George scrolled down to the last page and read, Today I met two people; George and Cynthia in Starbucks. She looked so much like my great-great-grandmother's friend, Cynthia. So, I questioned them and found out that they are time travelers and she is that good for nothing that gave Ruth so much trouble when she was alive. But, much to my surprise, they hired me to help them find a killer which I will do. But, I will make sure Cynthia is the murderer and get her out of the way. Then, I will use my feminine wiles to persuade George to marry me. When he is head over heels in love with me. I'll give him a sleeping pill and push him through his time machine to the old west. Then, I will have his time machine for my research. This payback is going to be loads of fun. However, whoever killed Art, I don't know and I don't care.

My sides hurt were several pieces of hot metal that Art was working on fell off the table and landed on me, while Art and I were messing around on the floor."

George read the last entry in Ruthie's journal that said, On a personal note. I think that Art is a great man even though he hit me on my jaw and knocked me out. But if he cheats on me he is going to feel my wrath.

Cynthia closed the Bible, walked to George, looked over his shoulder at what he was reading. Then she stated, "Why that lying little snake in the grass. Ruthie has the motive, the means, and the opportunity to kill Art."

"But we hired Ruthie after we found Art dead in his lab. So how could she have murdered him?"

"Would we still have found Art stabbed to death in his lab if after we hired Ruthie, she went back in time and murdered him?"

"I don't think so," stated George, "Because Art was missing long before we hired Ruthie."

"But if Ruthie changed the timeline when she killed Art, our memories concerning the case would have changed too," stated Cynthia.

George held his head saying, "Can we change the subject? All this talk on time theory is giving me a headache."

Cynthia printed out Ruthie's Journal and outlined in red where she wrote that she was going to pin the murder on her so she could marry George. Picked up the Arch Communicators saying, "Come on Babe, we have to talk to Ruthie. Then set the Time Arch for Ruthie's bedroom 7 hours into the future.

As they exited the Arch, Ruthie sat up in bed clad in her light blue baby doll PJs, and screamed, "How about some privacy!"

Cynthia threw a dark green lacy bathrobe at her and said, "Put it on and meet us in your kitchen."

"Its five in the AM!" roared Ruthie, "So I am going back to sleep."

"You either get out of that bed right now or I'll drag you out by the hair of your head!" hollered Cynthia.

"Alright, alright, just don't get your knickers in a knot."

Sitting at the table in Ruthie's kitchen, Cynthia gave her a red mug of coffee then asked, "Did you lose your smartphone?"

"Yeah, how did you know?"

Cynthia tossed it to her saying, "We found it in the dirt at Rubin's place. Care to explain? While you are trying to come up with an excuse, kindly tell me how you became an expert in the Time Arch so fast?"

"When we arrived at Rubin's place, I reached for my note pad in my purse and my cell phone fell out and I am a fast learner."

"Interesting answers. But tell me why do you want to inflict physical injury on me because of what Ruth told you? And I did not kiss that officer, Ruth did."

"Hey, have you been reading my journal?"

"Yes, and that brings me to my last question. What makes you think that you can take my husband from me so you can have the Time Arch!" screamed Cynthia. She then hauled Ruthie out of her chair by her robe, got in her face, and stated, "I have a half a mind to open an arch to the US in1520 and banish you there. For what you tried to do to my husband and me."

George calmed down his wife, then questioned, "Ruthie, what happened? Once you use to follow the Lord. Now all you can think of is fame and fortune." He showed Ruthie the picture of the sunrise at Rubin's cabin then stated, "This photo tells me a lot. Now, get yourself right with the Saviour before you wind up in big trouble. Oh, you didn't drop your cell phone when you reached in your purse because it was damp as if it had been lying there for a day or two, which tells me that you have been using my Time Arch without my permission, and I am not going to question you what you were doing at Rubin's cabin. Because your actions tell me exactly what you and Reuben were doing, and, if you are thinking of destroying my Time Arch. I have installed a failsafe system that will send 50,000 volts into the individual who tries to destroy the Arch."

Ruthie stared at George then stated, "Your house is hooked up to regular street power so there is no way you can generate that much electricity."

"I had three step-up transformers built into the arch. Now, get ready because we have to question Don Hollister."

"Can I take a shower first?

"Sure,"

While Ruthie was showering, she let go of a long loud bloodcurdling scream, then shouted, "Who turned off the hot water?"

Cynthia sat at the table trying to look innocent, George asked, "Sweet. What did you do?"

"Not much. I just turned off the hot water."

"You have got to stop teasing Ruthie."

"Not to change the subject but why are we still using her when she can turn on us?"

"Since Ruthie knows about the Time Arch she can cause us big problems and arrange the timeline so we don't meet her isn't an option because the timeline will change and foul things up for us."

Ruthie marched up to the kitchen table soaking wet, her hands clenched by her side, and a white fuzzy bath towel wrapped around her and stated, "Cynthia, you are obnoxious for turning the hot water off on me."

Cynthia stated in mock innocence, "Me. Do a horrible thing like that? Never. Ruthie, I think you should switch to decaf because you are too stressed out."

After Ruthie let go of a loud scream in frustration, George suggested, "You're dripping water on your floor so why don't you finish your shower."

"I would but somebody who shall remain nameless turned off the hot water!"

Cynthia stated with a smile, "Nameless would like to say something. Ruthie, if you try the hot water, you will see that you have plenty of it."

Ruthie took a fighting stance saying, "That's it! You, and me right here and now!"

George warned, "Ruthie, may I remind you that all you have on is a towel."

"Who cares!" screamed Ruthie then stated, "Come on Cynthia, I'm gonna kick the snot out of you!!"

George shook his head in disgust, excused himself, and went outside for a breath of fresh air. Cynthia approached her husband six minutes later saying, "Ruthie will be ready in about ten minutes."

"What happened?"

"You know how fussy Ruthie is about keeping things clean. I spilled the sugar on the floor, and when she bent over to clean it up, I grabbed the Taser from the counter and shot her in the derrière."

"Ouch. So, that was the thud I heard. Are you finished tormenting poor Ruthie?"

"For now. But if she gets out of line again, I have a whole arsenal of things ready to use."

Around nine minutes later, Ruthie approached George clad in a brown and black Bicycle Suit, that women wore around 1890, long black stockings and black shoes that went a quarter way up her legs, and stared at him with a scowl and said, "Are you happy? I put on this clown suit that you wanted me to wear."

"Those holy jeans of yours were drawing attention. Besides, women and jeans did not go together in 1890 and women did not begin to wear jeans for an everyday dress until 1960. Of course, you can wear the bright red bloomer Cynthia gave you."

"I wouldn't be caught dead in those things."

George stated, "Cynthia Sweet, open a Time Arch to your place in 1891 around ten in the morning."

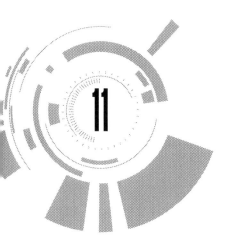

11

Interrogation

At Cynthia's home in 1891, she served coffee and chocolate chip cookies to Ruthie and her husband. When Don Hollister boldly walked in the back door clad in dirty work clothes and messy hair, grabbed Cynthia around her waist and gave her a long hug and kiss. She pushed him away saying, "I would like you to meet my husband George."

Don stared at Cynthia with his mouth open in shock for thirty seconds before saying, "You are kidding me? You married him."

"I have been married to him for two months, didn't you get the wedding invitation?"

"It must have gotten lost in the mail. Anyways, fix me up some sausages, eggs, and home fries. Then you and I can take a walk."

George showed Don the marriage license and stated, "Cynthia is through jumping every time you say something, and no she is not gonna be taking a walk with you at any time. However, if you take a seat, I want to ask you some questions."

Don gazed at George and said, "Cyn, you are serious about this marriage thing."

"Yes, and the name is Cynthia."

After Don sat on the couch, Cynthia handed him a mug of coffee and George inquired, "What do you know about Art?"

"You mean Art Boulder. The one who has the lab under his barn?"

"That's my farm and I don't know about any lab under my barn," stated George.

"What did you do to evict him?" asked Don.

"He is missing and I was wondering if you knew anything about his disappearance?"

"Ask your wife. She dated him."

Ruthie asked, "Is it true that you threatened to kill Art after you two had it out in your home?"

"The guy is unreliable. Once, I asked him if he could pick me up some bread. He did. Three weeks later. If he says that he will visit you that day. You can count on him not showing up."

"But what was the fight about? Did you start it?" inquired Ruthie.

"Art forced his way in my house early one morning and demanded that I pay him the 86 dollars that I owed him. I told him that I didn't. He became agitated and gave me a shove. I pushed back and threw him through my front door. Art chargeback in my house and I clotheslined him, then dragged his sorry hide outside. From then on, he bugged me every day about the money. But I didn't owe him any money."

"So, you stabbed him in a fit of rage." stated Ruthie

"A knife is too messy, I'd a put a bullet between that Jerk's eyes."

George thought for a moment then said, "You and Cynthia go way back and you treated her as if she was your wife. But when Art began to date Cynthia, you saw red, and sought for a way to get rid of your rival."

"Art, a rival?" questioned Don, "You're pulling my leg, right? And when was Art murdered?"

"Sometime between 1885 and today." stated George.

"So, you don't have any clues or an idea as to who killed Art."

"I have a list of names as to who it was and you are close to the top."

Ruthie inquired, "Did you ever find the bone-handled hunting knife that you lost 6 years ago?"

"How can a little pipsqueak like you know so much? No,"

"Were you dating Ruth about that time?"

"What's it to you."

"Just tell me."

"Yes, I did and I'll never date her again."

"Your knife was used to kill Art Boulder."

"I didn't do it." Don set his gaze at Cynthia and said, "So, how about that walk?"

George stood, placed his right hand on Don's left shoulder saying, "What part of Cynthia is married, don't you understand?"

"it's hard to believe that she married the likes of you."

"Believe it because it is true."

Don stared at Ruthie for forty-five seconds, then said, "Now I know where I saw you. It was a Saturday afternoon and you were holding Rubin's hand as you strolled through that park."

Ruthie nervously stated, "You must have me confused with somebody else."

"No, I haven't, it was you alright because I will never forget your heart-shaped beauty mark on the left side of your upper lip."

Ruthie eyed George then slumped down in her chair praying that he would not say anything to her regarding the Time Arch.

Once Don had left, Cynthia stated, "Both Rubin and Don have good reason to kill Art, but I think we should investigate Ruth a little more. Because she is too squeaky clean for someone with her background."

Ruthie hollered in protest, "Wait a cotton picken minute! My great-great-great-grandmother is not a criminal."

"If you will excuse me for a moment I'll get my journal that I have kept since I was twelve and prove to you that Ruth is a shady character."

12

The Truth

Cynthia came back seven minutes later with an album that was two feet long and one-foot wide and four inches thick that had hand-carved flowers on a wooden cover. She opened to the first page saying. "My journal has pictures with writing. That first picture is me drawn by my mom who was a sketch artist. But you don't want to read about all my first when I was growing up."

Cynthia turned several pages, pointed to a newspaper clipping, and said, "When Ruth was eight years old, she ran away from home as you can read."

Ruthie stared at the journal and asked, "You had your first kiss from Don Hollister when you were ten?"

"Yeeeeah. Dad heard about it and grounded me for a week. When Ruth was twelve, she was expelled from school for cheating on a history test, and here is the note from the teacher to prove it."

"How did you get it?" questioned Ruthie

"Ruth showed it to me and I pocketed it."

"In other words, you stole it," stated Ruthie.

"Let's just say that I borrowed it and forgot to return it."

"Hey, you even have a newspaper clipping about Abraham Lincoln's election announcement. Far out, Oh, hey there is a clipping about the beginning of the Civil War."

Cynthia turned the page, pointed to a newspaper article about a bank robbery, and asked, "Do you recognize the people in the photo?"

"Yeah, that's Art and Ruth. Was she a hostage?"

"Read the article and find out," stated Cynthia.

After Ruthie read the piece she stated, "It had to be a misprint, because it says that Ruth was the one who drove the getaway car."

"That's no misprint. Oh, and that's a photo of Ruth's dad in the Confederate Army ready to fight in the civil war and he was never heard from again. In 1871 Ruth's mother worked in a cotton Mill to put food on the table. So, me, conning Ruth's family out of their hard-earned money is a lie."

"But Ruth told me that her father was wealthy and you swindled him out of his riches."

"Here is proof that my mom and dad were wealthy and left it all to me."

"Oh, Buffalo patties." muttered Ruthie, "I am in so much hot water."

George inquired, "Ruthie. Do you want to talk about it?"

"No, it's something that I have to figure out by myself."

Cynthia glared at Ruthie and inquired, "How did you know that Don lost his hunting knife six years ago when I didn't even know? Did you use the Time Arch without my husband's permission?"

"Me, use the Time Arch and not ask George? Never."

"Then pray tell how did you know?"

"It was a wild guess." stated Ruthie smiling.

Cynthia stated, "If you notice I am not smiling. Now out with the truth."

"Okay, when you, George, and I were at the hotel and your husband sent me back to the Time Lab. I took a detour to Don Hollister's place late one afternoon on July 24, 1885, to ask him some questions about Rubin. The Time Arch opened on the right side of his farmhouse and I heard people talking and walked in the backyard, hid on the side of his house, and heard Art telling Don about the great weekend he had with Ruth. That's when Don told Art that he lost his bone-handled hunting knife. After Art left, Ruth exited the backdoor of the house, slip the knife in her purse, gave Don a long kiss, and rushed away."

Cynthia stated in disgust, "I knew that good for nothing was seeing another woman behind my back. Sorry for grumbling, but that puts the murder weapon in Ruth's hands."

George stated, "Ruth maybe a lot of things, but I don't think she is a killer besides, she doesn't have a motive for killing Art."

George gazed at Ruthie and questioned, "Can you explain to me again how Art tied you up after he tried to get fresh with you?"

"Art gave me a hard-right cross to my jaw, knocking me down then he belted me in my face knocking me out. I came too tied up and gagged under the cot."

George opened the Time Arch and sent Ruthie back to her home, saying, "Get some rest and I'll see you tomorrow morning for breakfast."

With Ruthie gone, Cynthia asked, "Babe, do you have Ruthie's Time Arch Communicator?"

"Yes, I made sure she didn't take it with her so I slipped it out of her purse when you were talking to her. Let's go back to our time and check the clues that we found in the lab, maybe we can find something that will tell us who put them there and why."

In the lab under the barn in 2020, George took a picture of Cynthia's left shoe with the nick in the heal and the photo of her wearing the same shoe. He uploaded them on his computer and projected them on a white movie screen. Enlarged them then scrutinized the missing button on both shoes and stated, "The shoe you are wearing in the photo. The threads that held the button on are ragged As if the button was ripped off, and the shoe that we found in the lab the threads are smooth as if it were cut off. The nick in the heal of the shoe we found in the lab appears as if it was carved out with a knife while the one you are wearing in the photo is ragged. This means the shoe we found in the lab was put there to make it look like it was yours."

Cynthia picked up the piece of cloth that looked like it was torn from her dress and stated, "I can show you the dress that has the same pattern on it but there isn't a tear anywhere on the dress."

George stated, "I know it's unpleasant for you to remember what happened when you were in the lab with Art. But is there any detail you forgot that could link the killer to Ruth?"

Cynthia examined the torn fabric than stated, "This material was not manufactured in 1885."

"Are you sure of that?" question George.

"When I lived in 1890 I was a woman of fashion and I made it my business to know what type of fabric my clothes were made out of. This piece of material came from 2020, not 1890. I just remembered something, Ruthie stated that Art gave her a right cross to her jaw. Art is left-handed because he lost 80% of the use of his right arm when he was cutting down a tree. Which means Ruthie lied to us again."

George stretched and stated, "It's getting late Sweetheart. What do you say we call it a night and start first thing tomorrow morning."

"Before we dive back into who killed Art I have a couple of bags of antiques I want to give to Frances. But I have to say this, the murder weapon can be traced back to Ruth, and the torn material can be traced back to Ruthie. Could those 2 have conspired together to take out Art?"

George moaned, "I came across a file that proved that Ruthie and Art were fulling around on the lab floor when some things hot from the table fell on Ruthie giving her those injuries. But right now, all I am thinking of is sleep."

The next morning around 9:30 AM, Cynthia inquired, "Babe, what did you do with the references that Ruthie gave you concerning her working for us?"

"I was going to do a follow-up but I was distracted by Ruthie constantly bombarding me with all kinds of questions about my heritage."

George glanced at his watch then said, "Ruthie should have been here an hour ago. Sweetheart, could you give her a call to find out what's holding her up?"

Cynthia returned 5 minutes later and stated, "Ruthie doesn't answer her phone so I sent her a text message but she didn't reply. I'll go to the Time Lab to see if she accessed the Time Arch without permission again."

Cynthia returned 20 minutes later, poured herself a cup of cinnamon tea, and stated, "Ruthie's Arch Communicator is missing. So, I checked the back up on the computer and Ruthie went back in time to 1886 to talk to Ruth. So, I locked out her Arch Communicator so she can't get back."

"Shall we question some of Ruthie's friend?" asked George.

"Sure, but let's stop at DDs for coffee before we go."

Some twenty minutes later, George parked his car in DDs, took a swallow of his Hazelnut coffee and stated, "The first person that Ruthie put down as a reference is Tracy Sanchez and lives on 518 Lauren Avenue, Knoxville."

An hour later, George parked his car in front of a beautiful red brick house, walked up to the door with his wife, and rang the Bell. A short young woman in her early 30s with dark brown curly hair, clad in holey jeans, and a dark blue button-down blouse, open the door, smiled, and asked, "Can I help you?"

George answered, "I'm looking for a Miss. Tracy Sanchez?"

"That's me is there something wrong?"

"Ruthie put you down as a reference and we would like to ask you some questions. Oh, this is my wife Cynthia."

"Come on in, I'll serve some coffee and snacks then we can talk."

They sat in a lovely living room with colonial furniture. Tracy served the refreshments and question, "What is it that you want to know about Ruthie?"

"How long have you known Ruthie?" question Cynthia.

"I bumped into her about 10 years ago in a shopping mall and we became instant friends. Going out for coffee, clothes shopping, you know doing girl things. But this past couple of months I haven't seen hide nor hair of her."

"Did you ever meet any of Ruthie's boyfriends?" asked Cynthia.

"No, because she could never be faithful to one guy If you know what I mean."

George inquired, "Have you known Ruthie to stretch the truth from time to time?"

"Truth, to Ruthie is a dirty word and will exaggerate the truth so she looks good."

"Why do you hang around a woman like Ruthie?" question Cynthia.

"I'm a writer, and Ruthie gives me a whole lot to use. So, I make mental notes of how I can put it in the story that I'm writing. Oh, one day I had my friend Donald at my house for the afternoon. Ruthie showed up and wanted to know if she could clean my house. I said yes. But she followed poor Donald around my home all afternoon and I had to stand guard in the hall so he could shower. When she finally left I had to get a towel and wipe Ruthie's drool off him, sort to say. Donald told me that the next time he came to my house he did not want to see her because Ruthie made him sick to his stomach."

Cynthia questions, "Does Ruthie have a temper, and do you think she could kill someone?"

"Ruthie drop by my house one Saturday afternoon to talk. I made a pot of coffee and we sat at the kitchen counter and she went into a rage, saying, "I put on my best dress, got all dolled up for Hugh and he had the nerve to turn me down! Just wait till the next time I see Hugh I'll tell him a thing or two! The way I feel right now so help me I would put a bullet in his head if I had a gun. But Ruthie never saw Hugh again because he was suddenly called home to be with the Lord."

"Didn't Ruthie know that Hugh had passed away?" question Cynthia.

"No, and she didn't care. Ruthie wanted what she wanted and nothing else mattered. I'm a little late in asking you this question but what is Ruthie to you?"

"She's doing some research for me," stated George.

"Ruthie is good at researching however, she'll find a way to use it for her selfish means."

Cynthia questioned, "Tracy. I look around your living room and see that you are a born again Christian. Why do you have Donald come to your house and shower when it's just you? Don't you think that's improper?"

"Donald was involved in a car accident a year ago, and they had to reconstruct his neck. The surgent told him that he should have someone around when he took a shower just in case he fell. So, I have Donald come to my house to take his shower and wash up without him worrying that something is going to happen when he is alone. Yes, there are times when I have to help Donald in and out of the shower. But he lives alone and spends most of his week in solitude because his friends just give him a quick high and by at church on Sunday. To turn my back on a brother in Christ that is in need would be a sin. I lost my husband 11 years ago in a plane accident. But by the grace of the Lord Jesus Christ, He has turned my morning into dancing. I spotted Donald struggling to get in his car one Sunday after church and decided to help him. Big deal, I've seen his bare derriere several times but it would devastate me if I knew Donald hurt himself in the shower when I refused to help. So, when he comes to my home to take a shower, I pray and ask the Lord for strength and wisdom, then when he is cleaned up he treats me to a meal at a diner."

Cynthia stated, "In other words, helping Donald takes your mind off of the loss of your husband."

"Yes, because true joy is Jesus, others, and yourself. By helping Donald, the Lord is teaching me how to be a servant. When I first met Donald that day in the church parking lot, I took him food shopping, then brought him home. Donald got in a manual wheelchair as I helped him put away his groceries. That's when he asked me if I minded hanging around while he showered. I was about to turn him down when the thought hit me, *"How would I feel if he fell in the shower when I said no."* I felt funny being in his house when Donald was in the shower, but he needed help and I determined in my heart to be there for him. I then made sure that Donald was safely in and out of the shower. Oh, I also clean his house every Saturday morning then we sit on his back patio, drinking coffee and sharing the scriptures."

George showed Tracy a picture of the morning sky taken at Rubens cabin and questioned, "What is the first thing that comes to your mind?"

"Ruthie has told me countless number of times that she hates getting up at the crack of dawn to go to somebody's house. If she took this picture of the morning sky at Ruben's cabin, you better believe she spent the night with him."

Cynthia inquired, "Have you ever shared the gospel with Ruthie?"

"Ruthie professes Christ in her life but she is struggling in her walk. Is Ruthie in any kind of trouble?"

"She is a suspect in a murder case but the evidence against her is weak. My wife and I have got to go and talk to the others that Ruthie put down as references. Here's my card, please keep in touch."

13

Checking up on Ruthie

In the car, Cynthia stated, "The next person on the list is Sarah Peters at "1431 Jourolman Avenue."

Around twenty-five minutes later, George parked his car in front of a pale yellow bungalow, Cynthia rang the doorbell and a tall willowy woman with short light brown hair done up in a pixie, clad in a tan skirt and a red short sleeve blouse. Silently stared at Cynthia then stated, "If you are selling something I am not buying."

Cynthia asked, "Are you the Miss. Sarah Peters, who owns the yellow, 2020 Lamborghini Murcielago that I have heard so much about?"

Sarah let go a belly laugh and said, "If I owned a car like that I would not be living here. Come on in."

Sarah brought George and Cynthia to an ultra-modern living room, served them iced tea in a tall frosted glass.

Cynthia asked, "Do you know a Ruthie Susan White?"

Sarah almost choked as she took a swallow of her iced tea and asked, "You mean that thing that runs around pretending that she is an expert in Genealogy?"

"Yeah, that's her. I try to avoid that woman at all costs."

"She seems harmless. Why the hostility?" question Cynthia.

"That thing is far from harmless. For one, every time she sees me she has her hand out for money. She then tries to tell me that she could research my family tree better than anyone in the world. I told her that I had a great genealogist and he doesn't charge high prices."

Cynthia asked, "Would you say that Ruthie is devious."

"Ruthie maybe dishonest, unethical, treacherous, immoral, underhanded, two-faced, but devious, no."

Cynthia stared at Sarah lost for words for a minute then questioned, "What happened between you two?"

"It was Bagel Sunday after church in the fellowship hall, Ruthie approached me about doing my family tree. We talked about my family tree until they began to fold up the tables and chairs. The next day, Ruthie came to my home and worked on my computer for most of the day researching my family. But came up with; nil, zilch, not a single thing, nothing at all, not even a dicky bird, not anything, diddly-squat, bupkis, naught, none. However, when I logged online to check my bank account, it had diddly-squat, a zero balance, like there was nothing in it, Zilch and there was no way I could trace who did it and where all my money was transferred to."

"How much was missing if you don't mind me asking?"

"Twenty-two thousand dollars. I reported it to the bank and they restored my money, but from then on, I stay clear of that evil woman."

Cynthia questioned, "Are you sure Ruthie took your money and not some online hacker?"

"I logged on that morning to make a deposit and when I checked after Ruthie left, my checking account was dry, nothing in it, completely drained, as in empty."

Cynthia inquired, "Have you seen Ruthie handle knives?"

"During lunch, the day Ruthie was researching my family tree, she took two of my carving knives, threw them up in the air, caught them and sliced up the roast beef faster than anyone I have ever seen."

George inquired, "Would you say Ruthie has the ability to kill someone?"

"Definitely, without a doubt, unquestionably, for sure, yes, as in I am positive."

George shook Sarah's hand saying, "Thank you for your information. My wife and I will contact you if we need to ask you more questions."

"What did Ruthie do this time," asked Sarah.

"She may have murdered someone, but we are not sure," stated Cynthia.

"As much as I detest, hate, and despise and feel contempt for Ruthie, I will be praying for her."

Back in the car, Cynthia stated, "I think that woman needs to read something else besides that huge dictionary she had on her glass coffee table."

George chuckled and stated, "Maybe she was just trying to make sure that we understood her answers by using all those words."

"The next person on our list is Martha Dirtbottom at 320 East Caldwell Avenue. Cynthia giggled and stated, "I'm glad I don't have a last name like that. I bet that woman is constantly being ribbed about her last name. I wonder if her mother and father sat in the dirt a lot?" question Cynthia snickering.

George warned, "Don't even think about poking fun at her last name 'cause you'll blow our investigation for sure."

"I promise I won't, but boy is it ever tempting to throw a few digs in when we talk to her."

Some minutes later, George parked his car in the driveway of a white; one-story house that had a carport and an extension built on the back. A woman who was 5 foot 2, in her mid-20s. with shoulder-length dark, brown wavy hair answered the door clad in pea green shorts and a white short sleeve button down top.

George tried to keep from laughing when he stated, "Miss Dirtbottom. my wife and I would like to ask you a few questions about Ruthie Susan White."

The woman smiled and said, "And no, my parents never sat in the dirt in their bear tushies. Come on in and don't worry I'm used to all the jokes and puns about my last name and it doesn't bother me,"

Martha brought George and Cynthia to her back patio where they sat on a Wooden couch made out of Cedar. Martha served them lemonade in tall light blue glasses and bagels with cream cheese. She sat in a bright yellow Adirondack chair, took a sip of her lemonade, and stated. "I've known Ruthie when we were in kindergarten and she is a good, loving individual but she got in with the wrong crowd. Or should I say got involved with the wrong person. From day one, Ruthie's parents told her that no matter what happened in her life she had to do what she was told and not complain about it. When Ruthie was 18, she went out on her first date with a young pastor. He was an authoritative type of person that when he said something you had to do it or else. This pastor was also devious and cunning and tricked Ruthie into going all the way with him one evening at his house. From that point on, her morals went downhill and she became cunning and sly just like Pastor Larry Farnsworth. She developed an attitude: I can sin all I want as long as I repent. But the Word of God says; shall we sin that grace may abound? God forbid. I've tried to talk to Ruthie about the way she is living but she *won't* listen. In her eyes, Pastor Farnsworth's word is law and she obeys him no matter what the consequences. Not to tell stories out of school but Pastor Farnsworth convinced Ruthie to sleep with some of the married men in the church so he could blackmail them."

Cynthia asked, "And you know all this information about Ruthie because?"

"As I said, Ruthie and I have been best buds ever since kindergarten and she confides in me. Why just last week she called me early in the morning and told me about some guy by the name of Don Hollister and how much fun she had with him one weekend. I told Ruthie that she had to straighten up her life and stop sleeping around because one day it gonna bite her in the butt big time."

"Can you hit some of the highlights of Ruthies weekend with Mister Hollister?"

"Sure can. Ruthie said that Don showed her around his farm, they had a romantic dinner where he cooked up some luscious steaks, potatoes, and corn. But before they could turn in for the night, someone by the name of Art visited Don and screamed about a woman named Ruth and how she was using him to kill Cynthia for her money. But all Art was interested in was cuddling with Cynthia, but she wouldn't agree to it. Art smiled and said that he was going to buy her a nice pair of stockings with hopes that would put him on her good side so they could nuzzle."

"So, what you are telling my wife and I that Art and Don are close friends and both of them want to date a woman named Cynthia." stated George

"Did Ruthie say anything about the woman," inquired Cynthia?"

"Just that she was a prude, should have lived in the 1800s and couldn't understand what Don and Art saw in her."

Cynthia stated, "Maybe it was her demureness that they like."

"That's possible," stated Martha.

George inquired, "Did Ruthie say anything about Art being murdered?"

"No, she didn't. But Ruthie did say that Don and Art were bosom buddies and that he would not do anything to hurt his pal even though they were after the same woman."

Martha stared at Cynthia and said, "You're the woman that Don and Art were after. Then tell me this. Why are you flirting with 2 other men when you are married?"

"Art is dead, I don't have any contact with Don, and I have no idea what Ruthie was babbling about."

"Then you did date Don at one time." stated Martha.

Cynthia glanced at her husband and said, "We went out on one date and it was a night that I'd like to forget."

"You know it is not healthy to hold things inside because it will eventually come out in some form of sickness. Now out with-it sister," stated Martha.

"If you must know, it was the day after the harvest ball and I was still trying to get over what Art tried to do to me, when Don walked in the back door of my home dressed to the nines. Handed me some roses, then told me that we were going to paint the town red because he wanted to get serious with me. I was delighted and I was on cloud 9 all night thinking about how my life would change being married to Don. Around one in the morning, I was sitting in his car waiting for him when I spotted a letter. I opened it and found out that it was from a woman who shall be nameless. She was thanking him for the great evening they had at the harvest ball and was looking forward to spending Saturday at the fair with him, which was coming up. When Don got back in the truck, I screamed, "How could you lie to me like that!" I threw the letter in his face, got out of the truck, found a police officer, and had him escort me home. But Don was like the bad penny that always shows up. But, thanks to my hubby he stopped Don from bothering me."

Martha stated, "So you think Don killed Art for getting fresh with you."

"Something like that. Hey, we gotta go."

"Before you guys go, could you pray for me? I am on the go from morning till night seven days a week. I was on my way out the door when you guys showed up. What I need the Lord to do is give me the strength to continue without dropping from exhaustion,"

Cynthia stated firmly, "What you should do is tell them that you have to take one day to rest. Then don't answer your phone, or text messages and go to a park and relax."

"But they depend on me."

"Will they be there for you when you are in the hospital from extreme physical and mental fatigue?"

"I can't say."

George stated, "Your body is the temple of the Holy Spirit. When you abuse it with food and junk it is wrong. It is just as wrong when you push yourself to the point of collapsing. Oh, Friday nights at six my wife and I are having a Bible study. You are welcome to join us."

"I can't, I have to work slinging hash at a truck stop."

"Can you take dictations, work on a computer doing research, and all-around office work?"

"Sure can, business was my major in college."

"It is in a top-secret lab so you will not be able to tell anybody what type of work you are doing. Oh, it also involves traveling."

"When do I start? I am tired of working around those crude truck drivers."

"It pays twice the amount of what you are getting at the truck stop."

"Just tell me when and I'll be there."

"Here is the address. Report to work tonight at 5 PM. and wear casual attire."

"Martha wrote Pastor Larry Farnsworth's address on a piece of paper and said, "This is just in case you want to talk to him about Ruthie."

"In the car, Cynthia asked, "Why did you hire her?"

"I plan to fire Ruthie, but I have to figure out how to do it without her telling the whole world about my Time Arch. Plus, Martha can keep an eye on her when we retrieve her from the past. Any more of Ruthie's referrals?"

"We have three left but I want to find a coffee shop and discuss the murder case."

George and Cynthia sat at a white round table in the HoneyBee Café in Knoxville. They ordered coffee Crumcakes. Cynthia took a swallow of her Vanilla Cream coffee and said, "I think we can cross Don off the list of suspects because of what I know about him and what Martha told us. He could not have murdered Art."

"I see you still have a soft spot in your heart for Mister Hollister." quipped George

"You have got to be kidding? Mister Hollister is the last man on earth I want for a husband and I would like to forget the things he did to get my attention. To answer your statement; no, I don't have a soft spot in my heart for that creep but I do forgive him."

"Do you wanna tell me what the things are that Don did that got you so upset?"

"No, I don't want to talk about the time Don took me to a private lake In the middle of nowhere and tried to get me to go swimming with him." stated Cynthia in disgust, "Now let's get back to the subject at hand."

"What was wrong with swimming with Mister Hollister when you both had bathing suits?"

"Babe, in1885 the women never went bathing with the men because it was considered improper and there was no bathhouse for me to change into my suit."

"Men and women swam together at the beach back then and you could have changed behind a Bush."

Cynthia doubled up her fist, shook it at her husband saying, "You want a fat lip."

George held up his hands saying, "Alright, alright I was just joking so calm down."

"The subject about Mister Hollister is a source spot with me, now can we get on with talking about the case?"

"What about Rubin? Do you think he could have killed Art?"

"I think Rubin would have pounded the snot out of Art instead of knifing him."

George took a bite of his Crumcake and stated, "We are forgetting one person. The one who tried to slice you up on the hauling road."

"If you wouldn't have come along when you did. He would have killed me."

"To be honest with you. He did."

"What?" hollered a shocked Cynthia."

"After I bought Art's farm, I researched all the unsolved murder cases back in 1890 and stumbled across a case where a woman was brutally mutilated by a knife wheedling maniac. So, I became her knight in shining armor."

"You mean I should have died at the hands of that lunatic?" stated a surprised Cynthia.

"Yes. Your clothes were in shreds, your face was slashed to pieces and there was at least a couple hundred stab wounds all over your body. The person that found you said that your facial expression was frozen in horror."

"I've walked that hauling road ever since I was a little girl and was never bothered or harassed by anyone. Other people have used it and they always confessed that they felt safe on that road. Who that person was, I don't know and I've never seen anybody like him around my neighborhood or at church."

"Which tells me that lunatic knew you would be on that road at that time. Because of the clothes he wore, it could have been a woman disguised as a man. But I think we need to go back to that road and find some clues."

"Do we have to?" question a skittish Cynthia.

"Yes, we do. and don't worry you are not going to be attacked again, that I promise you. But 1st we have to meet Martha and get her oriented into the Time Arch, then we have to retrieve Ruthie from the past."

"I would like to pay Pastor Farnsworth a visit."

"Do you wanna tell me why?"

"I want you to try and get him to stop seeing Ruthie because with him out of the picture, prayerfully she'll put her focus where it belongs, and that's on Christ."

"Then the next thing we do is visit the pastor."

14

Deliverance

George parked his car in front of a luxurious ranch house on Clifford Street in Knoxville, greeted a short man clad in torn jeans, and a deep blue t-shirt working in a vegetable garden. He stood and said, "Can I help you, Sir?"

"Are you Pastor Farnsworth?"

"Yes, I am. Who are you?"

"I'm George Bentwood, and this is my wife, Cynthia. We would like to speak to you about Ruthie White."

"What about her?"

"I want you to break all communications with her,"

"Do you have a reason?"

"I am tired of you corrupting her morals and using her for your own, selfish means."

"Do you have proof that I am doing those things?"

"I am sure I could get some of the men to testify that you are blackmailing them and can get Ruthie to testify how you are abusing her."

"Go ahead and try. I'll even give you their phone numbers, but they're not going to say anything and neither is Ruthie. So, you and your wife can turn yourselves around and get off my property and stop wasting my time."

Cynthia got in the pastor's face and stated forcefully, "You've been warned; stay away from Ruthie. Be on the next bus out of Tennessee or, there's going to be trouble."

"Are you threatening me, lady?"

"No. the trouble you will be receiving will be from the Lord, not me, so heed my warning or pay the consequences."

As George and Cynthia turned to go, Pastor Farnsworth let out a scream, grabbed his right leg, then fell to the ground. George quickly spun around to see a deadly Northern Copperhead slither away. He called 911 then ministered aid to the pastor. But the snake's venom quickly spread through Mister Farnsworth's system and was escorted into the presence of the Lord to answer for his actions."

George stared at his wife with his mouth open in shock, then stated, "Remind me not to tick you off."

"I just told him what I felt the Lord wanted to say to him, I had no idea that my Lord and Savior would act that quickly. If you don't mind, I need a hug right now because that shook me up quite a bit."

After the ambulance took the pastures body away, George and Cynthia told the police officer what happened.

Back on the farm, George served his wife a cup of herbal tea in the parlor. Sat next to her and stated, "You should not keep all that anger inside of you because sooner or later it's gonna come out in some form of sickness like cancer."

"You are right Babe. As you know, Don would barge in my home early in the morning and drag me out of my nice warm bed. Yes, Don would whack me on my derrière every morning and say, "Woman, make me my breakfast." Sometimes I was able to put my housecoat on before I cooked his meal. But I never dressed until after he left for obvious reasons. I already told you what he does to me when I meet him in town. In other words, Don tried everything he could think of to get friendly with me tickling, kissing, snuggling on the couch, back rubs. It made me sick to my stomach every time he took off his shirt in front of me. When he took me out on that date, I thought I could handle his loud, obnoxious attitude, but I couldn't. But what drove me up the wall, he would rub his rough whiskers on my face that would turn my skin red."

"Did you ever tell him how you felt when he would annoy you."

"Are you kidding? How do you tell something like Don to go jump in the lake?"

"So, you kept it locked up inside you all these years and now it is coming out in fits of anger."

"Yeeeeeaaaahhh."

"What you need to do is forgive Don, and all that he had done to you, release him then, ask the Lord to forgive you. Because He is faithful and just to forgive us of all our sins. Then every time that anger rises, lift it to the Lord because we should cast all our cares on Him for, He cares for us."

At five that afternoon, George greeted Martha, who was dressed in tan slacks and a pink top. Took her into the barn with his wife, shoved a broomstick handle in the floor opening the stairs.

In the Time Lab, George programmed a Time Arch Communicator and told Martha that every time she entered the Arch she had to have her communicator with her.

Martha stared at George and stated, "I think your fancy arch is cool but time travel exists only in the movies. Now, show me what I have to do."

Cynthia asked, "If you could go back in time. Where would you go?"

"The afternoon of May 23, 2004, the park in Knoxville. My dad took me there and was struck by a hit and run driver the next day."

George set the Time Arch and the three of them exited into a park on a sunny afternoon. Martha silently stared at a little girl frolicking with her father. Tears ran down her cheeks as the little girl ran into her father's waiting arms. She turned to George and questioned, "But how?"

"It's called, Time Arch."

"Oh, that little girl was me with my dad. Thanks."

George took his Time Arch Communicator and set it for a week after Ruthie went back in time to1886. Knocked on Ruth's front door. Ruthie opened the door and grumbled, "It's about time you guys got here."

Cynthia stated, "You know you are not to use the arch without permission."

Martha waved faintly at Ruthie and said, "Hi kiddo."

"What are you doing here?"

"I'm your partner in time."

Ruth walked up behind Ruthie and said, "It's you again. Ruthie, close the door because there is a foul stench coming from outside."

"I gotta go with them. Thanks for the clothes and a place to flop."

As soon as Ruthie closed the door she gave Martha a big hug saying, "I'm glad to see you, it's been about a month since we've got together and talked. Hey, what do you think of time travel?"

"I'll tell you later. Right now, I am too awestruck at everything that is happening."

Back in the time lab in 2020, George sat Ruthie in a chair, took her Arch Communicator, and stated, "You were told not to use the Time Arch on your own, but you went ahead and did it anyway. Remember, you work for me and you do what I tell you to when you're on the job."

Ruthie smiled then stated, "George, I know all about you and your ex-wife, why she divorced you and why you moved out of Massachusetts. I will use the Time Arch when I want and there is nothing you can do to stop me and I don't care who killed Art. Oh, Cynthia, I know all about your grandparents and the illegal way they made their money. I also know about your steamy relationship with Zacharia Jones and why you had to leave Tennessee for nine months. So, George, this is the way things are going to go. I will use the Time Arch when I want for my own research. But I'll still do your research on your childish murder case. If you disagree with me, I'll tell the government about your time travels. Oh, just FYI. there is an algorithm in the time computer that will prevent you from going back in time to when we met. So, there is no way you can get rid of me."

A shocked Martha stared at Ruthie in unbelief then asked, "Who are you? You're not the Ruthie that I've known all my life. You would never stoop to things this underhanded. These nice people gave you a job and introduce you to time travel and this is how you repay them. By stabbing them in the back."

"My eyes are open to the vast potential of time travel so; I am going to take advantage of it. No one, but no one is going to stop me, not even you, Martha."

Ruthie stood to her feet, twirled around, and said, "Ruth gave me this skirt so I shortened it. What do you think?" and began to giggle.

Cynthia pointed to something on the floor that caused Ruthie to bend over. When she did, Cynthia quickly pulled up Ruthie's skirt, and shoved a needle full of a sedative into her rump. Ruthie quickly straightened up, turned around and hollered, "How dare you!" and collapsed on the floor out cold.

George picked Ruthie up, put her in the chair, and questions, "What did you do that for?"

"She's drunk or high on something plus, I was tired of listening to the garbage coming out of her mouth. George put her in the spare bedroom and let her sleep it off. Martha, could you keep an eye on her for me please so she doesn't wander off and hurt herself."

Several hours later, George and Cynthia were sitting on the new patio that they had built. George took a swallow of his iced tea and questions, "Do you wanna tell me about this guy Zachariah Jones and what happened to the baby you gave birth to?"

"There is no Zachariah Jones and I did not get pregnant. Do you wanna tell me why your wife divorced you and that you snuck down here to Tennessee to live?"

"I already told you that my wife Betty was involved with another man, got rid of me, and married him. But all that garbage that Ruthie was saying, is dribble and nothing more. I'm sorry I asked you about Zachariah because I already know that you were morally straight your whole life, and no I didn't check up on you. Because as a Christian you couldn't do those things and walk with the Lord at the same time."

Just then, Ruthie charged out the back door in her bare feet, twirled around saying, "Weeee, I'm flying!"

Martha raced out of the back door, tackled Ruthie, then said, "Sorry Boss, I turned my back for a minute and she was gone."

"I'll get some rope and tie her to the bed," stated George.

The next morning around 10:35 AM, Ruthie staggered to the breakfast table clad in an orange bathrobe with white frills. Sat down, put her head in her hands and moaned, "How did I get back here? Please answer softly because my head feels like somebody's playing the anvil chorus on it"

Cynthia stated, "We found you at Ruth's house in 1886. We brought you back here. And you proceeded to dictate to us how you were going to use the Time Arch. Then you blurred out a whole bunch of garbage about Zachariah Jones and things like that. So, I harpoon you in your tush with a sedative. Several hours later, you were running around the backyard stating how you were flying. Martha had to tackle you and George strap you to the bed to prevent you from hurting yourself."

"Sorry for using the Arch without permission. But I just had to talk to Ruth and she introduced me to something called Laudanum. I took one sip and the lights went out. Then I'm waking up in bed strap down with Martha staring at me. Oh, after Martha on tight me, she crawled into bed and was out like a light."

"What would you like for breakfast" question Cynthia

"Three Italian sausages, home fries, three eggs over easy, and Italian toast with marmalade on it and a large cup of coffee, black."

Later, Cynthia sat at the kitchen table with her cup of hot coco tea and stated,

"Ruthy, while George is working in the time lab, I need to talk to you. Your actions ever since we hired you have been deplorable and it's only by the grace of God that you're still working For us."

"Can you excuse me for a few minutes I have to make a phone call."

"Are you going to call Pastor Farnsworth?"

"Why yes, how did you know?"

"He died of a snake bite a couple of days ago. Here is the obituary if you don't believe me."

After reading the obituary of the pastor, Ruthie tore out of the house and up into the field crying. Cynthia caught up with her several minutes later and explained, "I am so sorry but that pastor wasn't doing you any good."

"You do have a point, being with that pastor was more or less my time of torment. But how much does Christ interact with our lives? Or does he just watch us from a distance?"

Cynthia stated, "When I was younger I broke my leg, tension slowly mounted as I tried to keep up with helping my mom after dad died. I tried to keep my focus on Christ but it was difficult because of everything that was going on in my life and me walking with a cane hindered things greatly. Then the weekend of the 4th of July, I headed for Rest N Nest Campground to relax with my friend Larry. That evening, I fell asleep in my cabin, and the Lord carried me away in the spirit. I found myself walking down a road on a cold, clear winter day with the presence of the

Lord permeating my surroundings. The fields were heavy with snow and were piled along the side of the road. I was like a kid full of joy in my heart and a smile on my face as I darted about saying, "Lord, this place is beautiful. With my dark green mittens on, I reached down and grabbed a handful of snow. I could feel and hear the cold snow crunch in my hand as I squeezed it. My sense of awareness was sharpened far beyond my understanding. The need to use reasonable force to defend against an attacker was gone from my life. I felt secure and protected and I did not want to leave. Then my horrendous problem of me helping my mom drifted into my mind. I fell to my knees, crying and pleading, "Please, Lord! Don't send me back because I can't do it!"

Everything within me wanted to stay with my Saviour and not have to deal with the horrendous problem of helping my mom when I needed assistance. Just before I woke up, the Lord told me that He had confidence that I would overcome. With the sense that I had just returned from somewhere, I could still feel the effects of the cold air on my face, as I lay in my cabin. But, there was something different about me. I had confidence that Christ was with me, and He would see me through my troubles.

Later, my friend Larry told me that there was a peace about me that was never there before. My inhibitions were gone, a spiritual and mental strength that I only dreamed of was turning inside me. It seemed as if I was inside, looking through a hazy window that muffled my hearing. It may not be a correct interpretation of scripture, that, says like looking through a dark glass. I then understood it to say that this world is out of focus and dark compared to Glory. That confidence that Christ put in me and the strength was exactly, what I needed to bring me through the hard trial that I had to face. So, you see Ruthie when we accept Christ in our lives, the Good Shepherd not only watches us but walked with us and gives us what we need to go through the trial. If Christ sees that, we're going to mess up, he'll carry us or bring us in his presence to strengthen us and refresh us."

Ruthie stared at Cynthia with her mouth open in amazement then asked, "Jesus actually did that? Whoa! I guess my walk with Christ has been pretty bad."

"It is gonna take time to walk out all the garbage that you have gotten yourself into. But I know you will do it."

"All that is going through my mind right now is confusion. By the way, what's George doing in the Time Lab?"

"Shall we find out?"

15

Martha digs up dirt

In the Time Lab, Cynthia inquired, "Babe. Have you figured out what you are going to use the room now that you have divided the Time Lab in half?"

"I attached a High-end Three-dimensional Transducer to the HJO Capacitor on the time Arch. That will send a signal to the subatomic emitters that will project a solid three-dimensional image in the Time recovery Room that I just built."

"In English Babe."

"I'll show you." George set the Time Arch for the hauling road early Sunday afternoon of August 10, 1890. Accessed the High-end Three-dimensional Transducer, then said, "Let's go into the Time Recovery Room and see what we have."

In the Time Recovery room were a three-dimensional image of the hauling road, the attacker, and Cynthia. George stated, "This frozen moment in time will allow us to examine the captured moment right down to the smallest detail. Plus, I can save the image in one of the 3, 500 terabyte storage unit. Ruthie, would you like me to show you what moment in time I froze when you were questioning Don?"

A nervous Ruthie stuck out her hands saying, "No, no, no! I think we should check out the hauling road scene first."

Martha opened the door to the Time room and asked, "Am I interrupting anything?"

"No." stated George, "You're just in time to inspect Cynthia's attacker."

Martha studied the attacker's footprints, followed them to a large fir tree, and stated, "The individual planned the attack because he hid behind this tree until Cynthia walked by which means the assailant knew her. Boss, can I open his shirt? I want to see if he has any tattoos on his chest."

Martha stood in front of the frozen image of the attacker, unbuttoned his shirt, and exclaimed, "Whoa! There's nothing, not even a body. Boss, why is that?"

"That's because the Time Computer and the Three-Dimensional High-End Transducer can only project what it sees. Since it didn't see a body it just projected clothes." George then stated, "Computer, scanned the image in front of me an add the proper features to the frozen image."

Seconds later, the frozen figure's upper body became visible and Martha stared at a woman's bare chest and shouted, "Whoa, he is a she!"

"Babe. Are you sure the computer is right?" questioned Cynthia.

"Positive, The Time Computer must have picked up some small details that we missed."

Cynthia stated, "Now that I think of it, my assailant's movements did remind me of a woman. But who? Babe, is there any way you can tell the time computer to remove the beard from the assailant's face?"

"Without something to go by, the computer cannot put the proper feminine features on the face. But we will have to do more investigating to see who the murderer is."

George faced the frozen image of Cynthia standing in front of the assailant and had the computer remove the image because it wasn't Important to the investigation.

Cynthia examined the assailant's clothes then stated, "All the tags and identifying markings have been removed, and she is wearing gloves which means the attacker had it all planned out, this means it was premeditated."

George stated, "In the original timeline, the attacker brutally murdered Cynthia, which tells me whoever she is, had a score to settle with her."

Martha asked, "Could it have involved a love triangle and the woman wanted to get rid of Cynthia so she could have the guy all to herself?"

"The only woman suspect is Ruth and both her and Cynthia were dating Art at the same time."

"Don't forget Ruth wanted my money and was willing to get it any way she could," stated Cynthia. She stared at Ruthie then stated, "The piece of fabric found in Art's Lab came from the year 2020. Sorry, Ruthie."

Ruthie smiled sheepishly and stated, "That piece of the torn dress came from me all right. George, when you and your wife were busy in town one afternoon. I used the Time Arch to go back to 1885 to give Ruth one of the dresses that I thought she would like. But I don't think my great-great-great-grandmother is the killer. Because Why would someone kill Art and then wait five to six years to kill her rival? We may be looking at two different killers. Cynthia, how many enemies did you have when you lived in the 1800s?"

"None that I know of."

Ruthie put her hand on her head and ask, "Sir, would you mind if I took the rest of the day off because my head is killing me and my stomach doesn't feel too good."

"Sure, take as much time as you need. I'll see you at breakfast tomorrow morning if you are up for it, if not, give me a call." George held out his hand and said, "Before you leave, give me your time Arch Communicator."

"Dang," muttered Ruthie under her breath as she handed George the communicator.

Martha questioned, "Ruthie, do you want me to give you a ride home?"

"Thank you but no thanks I can manage on my own," grumbled Ruthie.

After Ruthie left, Martha inquired, "Have you established the time of the murder?"

George stated, "The murder took place somewhere between 1885 and 1890. because I bought Art farm in 1890 he was already reported missing. But, I didn't find the victim's body until 2020 and all the evidence pointed to my wife being the killer. But in the light of recent discovery, we found out the evidence was planted to make it look like Cynthia was the murderer."

"Whoa! That won't do." stated Martha, "We have to find the time of death of the victim.

George stated, "It is impossible to know when the assailant stabbed Art because he was found 120 years later."

"There is an easier way," stated Martha. "When was Art Bolder reported missing and by whom? Then look up the one who put his farm up for sale."

Cynthia ran and to the house, got the papers of the sale to the house, and said, "Aron P. Shupe was the one who sold the farm." Cynthia thought for a minute then said, "Art Boulder's mom's maiden name was Shupe, and I think she lived west of here, in Farragut, Tennessee."

George answered his smartphone saying, "Mister B. How are you and Lauren doing?"

"Do you guys have time? Lauren and I would like to stop by for a few minutes before we head back north."

"Give Cynthia and me a minute and come on over."

Martha asked, "Company coming?"

"Yup."

Martha suggested, "Why don't you and your wife entertain your guests and I'll do the research."

Around seven minutes later, George opened the front door and greeted Mister B. and Lauren in her wheelchair. Then brought them into the Parlor. Cynthia served Apple Streusel Coffeecake and Coconut-Hazelnut flavored Coffee. Sat in the soft armchair and asked, "Mister B. can you tell me about yourself?"

"I sure can. I was born a pound and a half in a home in Nova Scotia, Canada that had no medical equipment to keep me alive. But by the grace of God, I survived and would have grown up a southpaw. But my mother thought it best to force me to use my right hand; this caused dyslexia, mental confusion, and the inability to function properly in school.

When I began to attend the one-room schoolhouse, the teacher took a disliking towards me for some unknown reasons and hit me on my arm every chance she got with a belt made from a car tire. My mother came to my rescue but, it was too late, I shut down emotionally because I hated school, and passed every grade on Special Consideration."

"I bet that strap hurt a lot," commented Cynthia.

"Every time she would hit me it stung like a bee. But being a quiet one, I never said a thing to my mom. At the age of sixteen, I made it to the eighth grade. Tired of being treated as a dummy I figured that I had all I needed in life; low self-esteem, negativism, lack of social skills, and the I Q of a stump I tried my hand at various occupations. But I found out that I was smart enough to wash dishes and push a broom, so that's all I did."

"Didn't you have any goals that you wanted to achieve?"

"No. My mom always told me that I was useless and I grew up without any male influence in my life. But because of several men's Bible studies, it changed all that thank the Lord. Back to what I was saying. At the age of 23, the doctor told me that I had a brain tumor and had six months left to live. However, before those six months were up, I received Christ in my life, and He gave me His Holy Spirit, which put new hope, and joy in my heart. However, my old persona followed me, convincing me that I was only good enough to warm a pew. That was it, the die was cast, I was a no-talent Christian and I settled down to be the best pew warmer I could."

Cynthia stated, "Christ gives all His children gift, so it is not them but the power of God flowing through them."

"You are so right," stated Mister B., "Anyway, some seven years later, my vision became blurred, my coordination was off and I was diagnosed with a brain tumor for the second time in my life. However, Christ delivered me from death's door again. But, two years later, death tried again by giving me a heart attack and I died. I woke in a shroud of darkness, experiencing a joy that cannot be put into words as I stared at a glowing red outline of the Lord Jesus Christ sitting on His throne. He told me in a deep voice, "Go back, for it is not your time." I am still here taking care of Lauren and serving my Lord and Savior."

"Give me a minute to pick my jaw up off the floor. That is an awesome testimony," stated Cynthia.

After an hour or two of fellowship, Mr. B. stated, "It's time Lauren and I hit the road because we have about 812 miles to home."

George stated, "Why don't you 2 stay here for the night and leave first thing in the morning. Don't worry about Lauren's wheelchair; we will take care of that."

Lauren stated, "You don't have to go through any trouble for us."

"Nonsense." stated Cynthia firmly, "You two are staying tonight, and that's that."

After a hearty breakfast, the next morning of sausage eggs toast and home fries, Mr. B and his wife headed North. George told Cynthia that he was going to finish researching Art's murder and left.

In the Time lab, George found Martha sound asleep slumped over the computer consul. She lifted her head, stared at him through blurry eyes, and asked, "Is it morning already?"

"You didn't have to spend the night here."

"Yeah, I did. Someone tried to access the Time Arch remotely last night around one in the morning so I shut it down."

"Did you locate who it was?"

"It was Ruthie. She must have snuck a spare Arch Communicator home with her. Don't worry Boss, I disabled it. Why she is acting like this I don't know."

"What else did you do besides catch some sleep?"

"I captured another moment in time in the Time Recovery Room and found something interesting. Let me show you. Oh, I know computerize and did a little reprogramming on the Time Computer. Now, when it captures a moment in time it will do an in-depth scan, which means It will pick up whatever is in a box, or a body underneath loose clothing."

Martha brought George in the Time Recovery Room and showed him Rubin's cabin that she had captured. Approached the frozen image of Ruthie clad in a purple halter top and hot pants talking to Rubin who was shirtless inquired, "Boss, did you fill Ruthie in on the proper attire of the 1800s?"

"That was the first thing I did."

"Her skimpy attire tells me that she got things going with Ruben. Now, look at her eyes and tell me what you see."

George stared into the eyes of Ruthie and stated, "They look exactly like the eyes of the one who tried to kill Cynthia."

"I have something else to show you in the cabin."

In the cabin, Martha opened a wooden box in a corner, took out some ragged clothes, a beard and mustache. Then asked, "Did Rubin hire Ruthie to get rid of Cynthia, if so, why?"

"I want to look into Ruthie's eyes again. We may be jumping to conclusions."

Outside, George gazed into Ruthie's eyes one more time saying, "These eyes also match Ruth's eyes. She is the same height as the killer and has a motive."

"But we have to connect Ruth to Art and Rubin. Then we'll have our killer." Stated Martha. She stared at George and inquired, "Boss. I am in a pickle and maybe you could shed some light on it. There is a man who lives three miles from me and has difficulty walking. I go to his house several times a week so he can take a shower and I make sure that he is alright."

"Are there any men that can assist him?"

"I tried to find one, but none of the guys are willing."

"What would happen if you didn't help him?"

"Since he lives alone, he could fall and hurt himself and there would not be anyone to come to his aid."

"As long as it doesn't lead into the flesh, I guess it is alright."

"I ah, have to help him in and out of the shower lots of times. Do you think it is alright for me to do that?"

"If your motive for helping him is compassion and not enjoy looking at his bare you know what. You should be good to go. But what does the Lord himself say?"

"Thanks, Boss. Oh, Boss. Last night I went outside for a breath of fresh air. When I came back in, I leaned against the inside of the barn wall by the picture of the horse and this notebook fell out of a hole in the wall. I checked it out and it's the rest of Art's journal. The first page read; October 4, 1885, I started this journal right after Cynthia walked out on me when I tried to get her to cuddle with me on the cot. I hid my journal so that pain, where I sit Ruth, doesn't see what I am writing. For one, Ruth is overbearing and I don't want her to know about, Maybell Fits. A woman my age who is cute as a button and lives in Abingdon, Virginia. So, for the next three months, I will be there having a ball.

"Interesting, does he write anything about Ruthie?"

"A whole lot, she was aggravating him by asking all kinds of questions about Ruth."

"What did you find out about Mrs. Shupe?"

"Art's funeral was on March 14, 1890, and she put his farm up for sale a week later. Oh, the funeral was a closed casket. I tried to locate where the funeral was held but I couldn't. I then got Mrs. Shupe's address, went back in time to talk to her. But she wouldn't tell me anything about Art. Oh, Art also wrote in his Journal, while Ruthie was asking me questions about Ruth. She walked in, saw Ruthie's skimpy attire, and thought that I was cheating on her. Which was true. Because when I saw Ruthie wearing practically nothing, I took off my shirt. The next thing I knew, Ruthie and I were on the floor fooling around. I am just thankful that we were not caught by Ruth when she walked in or she would have killed us. However, Ruth screamed at Ruthie for an hour about her being a Trollope, hit her across the face with a piece of wood that was on the table, and knocked her out. I left to get a wet cloth for Ruthie but she was gone when I returned. Ruth and I then went for a long walk.

George stated, "Martha, I want you to find out what type of relationship Ruthie had with Ruben and Don. then I want you to do some research on Miss. Fits."

"Yes, Boss I'll get on it right away."

16

Callie and Bo

Just then, Cynthia walked in the lab with a five-foot-five tall slender woman, with short wavy black hair and stuck her hand out for a fist bump.

George grabbed her fist and shook it saying, "Callie Swanson! How are you doing? Are you still writing those murder mysteries?"

Callie stared at her hand for a brief moment wondering why George didn't give her a fist bump then stated, "I just finished writing a book called 'The ill-fated trip to Denver.' And my last name is not Swanson anymore it's Sidewinder. I met Bo Sidewinder when the girls and I were traveling to Denver, we hit it off so well we were married several months ago."

"Congratulations, and I pray that you are enjoying your marriage. Oh, this is Martha Dirtbottom my assistant and gal Friday."

Callie giggled and said, "Miss. Dirty Bottom, how do you like working for George?"

Martha didn't like the way Callie pronounce her last name and stated, "That's Dirtbottom." and tried to hold her temper.

Callie stared at the Time Arch and inquired, "What in the world is that?"

Before George could answer, Martha stated, "Is just a fancy wall decoration that George tinkered together one afternoon." She then stated, "I knew of a sidewinder but he was a snake."

"Cute, real cute," stated Callie. She then said, "Another name for dirt is, gossip. Did your family get your last name because of all the gossip they spread around their town?"

"Listen up Smart Mouth. My Boss hired me to work not to stand in front of an ex-streetwalker and exchange snide remarks. I went to the same college you did and I know all about your steamy affair with the professor, and the son you had because of your relationship with him. I also know about your affair with a guy when you work as a counselor at that summer camp. So back off with the digs on my last name or your name is going to be mud, that I promise."

"You know nothing about me so back off Garbage Mouth." snapped Callie

"I know you were valid Victorian of your class because of the evening extracurricular activities you had, Miss June."

Callie quickly turned to Cynthia and said, "It been a long trip and I am starved."

"George and I made a big pot of American Goulash last night so I'll throw some in the microwave for you, then brew a pot of coffee."

George kissed his wife and told her that he would see her at lunch. Turned to Martha and questioned, "Why are you against Callie?"

"That woman made my life miserable in college."

"Oh, How so?"

"Every guy I met when I was in college, she took away from me and it became a four-year struggle just to date a guy. Plus, what ticked me off the most, I was to be Valedictorian, Callie had some Geek mess up my marks and I barely passed. I know this because the president of the college contacted me three months after my graduation and told me what had happened. Plus, I can give you proof why Callie is known as Miss. June, but I do not want to get into that right now. But I think we should pay for Miss Fits a visit. She lived on 117 Valley Street in Abingdon, Virginia, and set the Time Arch for anytime in March of 1890.

After George checked the time back up log he stated, "Ruthie went in the past to March 10 and spent two days there. One day she spent in Knoxville the other was in Abingdon, Virginia."

"Hey, that's where Maybell lives."

George called his wife on her smartphone and said, "We have time to waist."

"Be there in a few minutes. Callie was just leaving to meet her hubby and the two of them are going to talk to Ruthie."

A few minutes later, Cynthia rushed in the Time Lab, clad in her usual 1890-time travel attire, George set the Time Arch for 2 AM on March 10. George, Cynthia, and Martha rushed out of the Arch in the back yard of Maybell's two-story red brick colonial house and heard a scream coming from the upstairs window. George kicked in the back-door, raced upstairs in time to see a man dressed in ragged clothes and a beard charge out of the bedroom, push them aside, and ran downstairs. George hollered, "You two ladies check Miss Fits. I'm going to catch the would-be killer!"

Cynthia turned on the light hanging from the ceiling and found Maybell in her bed with a knife in her chest. Martha pulled out the knife, ripped open the white nightgown, and applied pressure to the wound.

A terrified Maybell questioned, "Who are you people and how did you get in my house?"

"We heard you scream and thought that you needed help. Fortunately, the knife didn't go in too deep. Now hold still. Cynthia, brew some black tea and bring the tea bags to me."

Cynthia raced through the Time Arch, brewed the tea, ran back through the arch, and gave the warm tea bags to Martha. She put them on the knife wound and applied pressure hoping the tea would help stop the bleeding.

Later, George walked in the bedroom panting and said, "She got away but I think it if the same killer that attacked Cynthia."

Martha used the attacker's knife to cut the bottom half of Miss. Fits white nightgown in strips, bandaged the wound then put her left arm in a sling. After the women assisted Maybell with her clothes and brought her downstairs and in her sitting room. A loud banging on the front door caught everyone's attention. Alicia Albright, an excited woman five foot nine with short red hair rushed in clad in her long dark blue nightgown asked, "What happened?"

"Some idiot attacked me with a knife and these kind people chased him off and saved my life."

"My husband is going for help. Can I get you anything?"

"A cup of tea would be great."

George asked, "Miss Fits, what can you tell me about Art Boulder?"

Her eyes filled with tears as she stated, "I miss Art's sweet smile and funny stories. I want to attend his funeral but Mrs. Shupe will not tell me where it is being held. Anyways. Art was a great inventor and knew how to fix things around my home. He was also a fantastic cook and prepared fabulous meals for me. Back in 1885 Art hung around his neighbor, Don. The two of them went hunting and fishing together a lot. But Art got upset when Don told him his outlandish stories about some woman named, Cynthia and the number of times they snuck off to some secluded pond and went bathing together without anything on. That's when Art stopped hanging around Don. But when Ruth started talking to Art about Cynthia, he suspected that Don Hollister had some devious planned, and wanted to use Art to date Cynthia so he could kill her and take her money. Art did date Cynthia which lasted for about 8 months until she dumped him. Ruth, who was having an affair with Don, was up-set that Art didn't follow through with the plans. She then took matters into her own hands and withdrew Cynthia's money out of the bank and gave half of it to Mister Hollister.

"Did Art ever talk about a Ruth White?" question Cynthia.

"Art talked about her all the time which would upset him. But I knew how to help Art to relax without getting into the flesh."

"What were some of the things Art mentioned concerning Ruth?"

"Ruth would tell Art that she would be at his place at a certain time and pull a no-show. Ruth was married when she was in her teens, but he died of a gunshot wound. But would always bring up what she did with him when she was married to him which bothered Art greatly. Art tried to get Ruth to clean his house but she never did a proper job and he referred to her like that, overbearing piece of work."

"Did Art ever mention a woman by the name of Ruthie?"

"Does she wear clothes that showed most of her bare body, has blond hair that she wears in a ponytail?"

"Yes, that's her."

"She visited me two weeks ago and wanted to know what my intentions were concerning Art. I told her that it was none of her business. Why? Is she the one who stabbed me?"

"Yes. But don't worry she will not bother you again, that I promise." stated George.

Maybell stared at George, feeling dejected and inquired, "Did Ruthie kill Art, the love of my life?"

"I think so," stated George. He looked at Alice and said, "We have to find the attacker. Could you take care of Maybell?"

"Yeah sure, she can live with us until she is back on her feet."

To save time George took his Arch Communicator out of his pocket, set it for a sidewalk restaurant in Knoxville, Tennessee 2 hours into the future.

Sitting at a round, black rod iron glass top table, George in the two women ordered hot tea and ice cream sundaes. Martha slowly scanned the busy street with its horse and buggies and stated, "So this is what it is like living in 1890. I love it!"

Some 13 minutes later, Ruth walked by clad in a new fancy dress she bought from Saks Fifth Avenue. Closed her frilly beige parasol and sat at the table between Cynthia and Martha. She glanced at Martha and stated, "Feeding another poor slob I see. Oh, I'm glad I bumped into you. I'm having a garden party this Saturday afternoon and I would love for you and George to attend."

"Us poor slobs will not be able to make it. But I do want to ask you a few questions about Ruthie."

"What about her?"

"Did she ever mention Art Boulder to you?"

"That's all she talked about was him and how fantastic he was."

"Did Ruthie ever ask you about your intentions concerning Art?"

"Yes, she did. She even went as far as asking me how many times I dated Art and if I ever got into it with him. I told Ruthie that I was after Don Hollister, not Art Boulder. Can I ask you a question, Cynthia? Since you're such a good friend of Ruthie. Why do you let her run around almost bare naked?"

"I'm not following you," stated a puzzled Cynthia.

"You know that small pair of pants and a little bit of a top she wears. Every one of my friends asked me why is she dressed like that. But I had no answers for them. So, when Ruthie was stuck at my house for a week I decided to give her some decent clothes."

Cynthia stared into Ruth's eyes and stated, "You and Don Hollister tried to get Art Boulder to kill me for my money, but all Art wanted to do was to get me in the sack. When he wouldn't kill me, you disguise yourself like me, went into the Wells Fargo Bank in Knoxville, and withdrew all my money that my mom and dad left me. You then gave Don Hollister half of it. But if you keep messing around with Don Hollister you're going to be a mommy. But what I want you to tell me is did you stab Art Boulder in a fit of rage because he wouldn't kill me when you tried to get him to do it."

Tears ran down Ruth's cheeks as she took off her white silk gloves and stated, "As you know I always wear gloves, that's because my hands are so chapped and sore and I have a hard time doing things. So, I get people to do things for me. Yes, I love Don but I go to his house several times a week because of ugly psoriasis all over my body. He puts me in a vat of hot mineral oil to try to cure me of these ugly red splotches. Then Don puts me on a table on my stomach and gives me a rubdown, loosening up my joints that hurt so much. If it weren't for him, I would be crippled up, unable to get around. Now you know my secret and I guess you're going to spread it all over Tennessee that Ruth White is crippled up with arthritis."

"How do you explain that you wanted to have Art date me so he could stab me?"

"Because I was poor and you had all that money I uh, lost my head. Sorry, if you're in need, I can give you a couple of $100,000.00."

"I forgive you Ruth but keep your money. The Lord Jesus supplies all my needs according to His riches in glory, which is something you should learn. So, you couldn't have killed art Boulder with the hunting knife because of your hands."

Martha placed her left hand on Ruth's shoulder and stated, "Let's pray that the Lord Jesus will heal Ruth of her psoriasis and chapped hands."

After the prayer, Ruth stated, "Wow! That's the first time I've ever felt that kind of peace. I promise every time Pastor Tumwater has a service I'll be there. Because whatever you have Cynthia I want it to. Hey, gotta go, it's time for my oil soaking."

At Don Hollister's farm a short time later, George knocked on his front door. He answered it saying, "You again! What do you want now?"

"We have to talk to you about Ruthie White."

"Make it fast because I'm gonna have company soon."

As they sat at Don's white metal kitchen table, Martha questioned, "We already know that you gave Ruth your hunting knife to kill Cynthia so you two could get her money. But Ruth couldn't do it because of her hands, so she tried to get Art to kill Cynthia for her. But all Art wanted was to snuggle with Cynthia. Did you knife Art out of frustration because he failed?"

"How could I kill Art when I didn't know Ruth has asked him to do it for her?"

"But Art was trying to take Cynthia away from you."

In mock innocence, Don said, "Cynthia washed my clothes, cooked my food, we went bathing together in our secret pond. But I never tried to kill her or Art."

Cynthia snapped back, "Don. Will you please stop telling people that I went swimming with you when I did not do it at any time!"

"You sure did because I always commented about that ugly dark brown mole on the lower part of your stomach."

"News flash Don. I don't have a mole on my stomach."

Don gazed at Cynthia for a few seconds then stated sheepishly, "You are right, it was Urina that I went swimming with."

A shocked Cynthia stated, "You went swimming with Urina? She's a midget and makes Ruth look fat. How could you get the two of us mixed up?"

"All you women look the same without your clothes on. Back to the knife. I gave Ruth the Knife because she told me that she had to cut up some deer meat."

"Give me a break for Pete's sake," hollered, Martha, "Ruth has severely chapped hands and couldn't hold the knife. Which you already know because you treat her. So, come up with another excuse."

"Okay, so I don't know why Ruth wanted my hunting knife."

George said, "Let's talk about Ruthie."

"Let's not. Okay," stated Don.

"Are you afraid that she will spill the beans on you?"

"No. All that woman can talk about is Art Boulder and how great he is. But she did ask me if Art was seeing anyone else."

"What did you tell her?" questioned George.

"I told Ruthie that Art was seriously courting Cynthia. That's when

Ruth screamed, I'll kill both of them so help me! Ruthie then stormed out the door. Sorry, Cynthia, I made it look like you and Art were into ah, you know. Hey, I wanted to make it look like Art was scoring with Cynthia."

Martha stated, "Ruthie has the motive, the means, and the murder weapon. All we have to do is put her at the scene of the crime and we have our killer."

17

Ruthie's Demise

Back at George's farm in 2020, Martha passed out in the den sound asleep, as Callie and her husband Bo, stopped by for a long visit. While they were sitting in the parlor talking over coffee and chocolate cake. Callie stated, "When I was in college some of us girls thought it would be fun to locked Martha outside in her short thin blue nighty. After that night, Martha had to take the week off from classes because all of the guys were teasing her."

Martha entered the parlor steaming mad, glared at Callie and stated, "You're despicable. Boss, Cynthia, I'm going home and I'll see you guys tomorrow morning. Oh, Callie, did you ever tell George what happened when you took a shower in the guy's locker-room." Martha smiled devilishly and said, "Later guys." And left.

A nervous Callie stated, "Hon, that's not the way it happened, honest. I was dating Dixon Paten at the time and he took my favorite fluffy pink bath towel in the men's locker for G and C. I went in, when the locker room was empty, took my bath towel, threw it around my neck and left. My friend Nancy saw me coming out and asked me if I showered in the men's locker room. Of course, Nancy spread it all around campus that I showered in the men's shower, but, from then on, all the girls at the college looked up to me because of what they thought I did and came out unscathed."

Callie's husband silently stared at his wife for a good minute, making her uneasy. She then shouted, "It's the truth, Hon honest!"

Bo smiled and said, "So you're Fancy Pants."

A puzzled Callie asked, "Huh?"

"I was in my senior year at that college when all the guys began to talk about a coed that took a shower in the men's locker room and they nicked named her Fancy Pants."

"You knew." asked a surprised Callie.

"Yes, and I know what kind of reputation you had around the college campus and I know why you are called Miss June because I've seen that calendar. But remember my little Cactus Flower. Now that you are in Christ, your past is under His Blood. Including Professor Nelson. That is Tommy's last name isn't it?"

"Y, ye yes, it is." Stated a shocked Callie.

"Good. When we get back, how about changing his last name to Sidewinder?"

"You mean it?"

"I sure do."

Callie stated with a gleam in her eye, "Just wait until we get back to the motel Mister, you are mine."

George stated, "Bo, you and your wife spent the day with Ruthie. How is she doing?"

Callie stated, "No matter how much Ruthie smiles, that woman is hiding something. Because she seemed anxious when she talked about a soon visit to a Miss Fits in Abingdon, Virginia."

George quickly rushed Bo and Callie out the door, called Martha saying, "We have time to waist."

"Be there in ten minutes, Boss."

In the Time Lab, George accessed the Time Records and discovered that Ruthie had overridden the Time Computer and went back in time to three in the morning of March 12, 1890.

Martha charged in the Time Lab with her hair a mess, cold cream on her face, her red button blouse partially open and half tucked in her white slacks, carrying her pink sneakers.

Cynthia helped Martha get presentable, and handed her a nine-millimeter pistol saying, "Ruthie is playing for keeps, so shoot to wound her."

George set the time computer for Ruthie's location in1890 and the three of them raced through the Time Arch, exiting in the back of a white stucco ranch. They heard a racket and screams from a woman coming from inside the house. They charged in and found Ruthie in the living room on the floor trying to stab Maybell. Martha pointed her pistol at Ruthie and hollered, "Don't do it!"

Ruthie stopped, stood up waving a long thin stiletto at Martha saying, "I don't want to hurt you. All I want to do is get rid of some garbage."

"Drop the knife Ruthie or I will shoot," demanded Martha.

Ruthie threw the knife at Martha and dove through the Time Arch she had used to access Miss. Fits home. George stared at the wall in the living room where the Time Arch was and hung his head.

Cynthia inquired, "What's wrong Babe?"

"I was in the middle of shutting down Ruthie's Time Arch when she dove through it."

"Meaning?" inquired Martha.

"Meaning, the Time Arch was in a state of flux and Ruthie is stuck in limbo forever."

Cynthia and Martha picked an unconscious Maybell up off the floor, dressed in a long pink nightgown, and set her on the couch. She opened her eyes 6 minutes later. Gazed at George, Cynthia, and Martha then said, "You people again. That woman came right through my living room wall and attacked me. Are you specters?"

George replied, "No ma'am, we are time travelers, and it looks like we stop a murder in time. The woman, Ruthie has been caught and she will not bother you ever again, that I can assure you."

"I just baked a whole bunch of brownies, so let me make some tea because I have a lot of questions I want to ask you."

Around 8:00 AM that morning George, Cynthia, and Martha bid goodbye to Maybelle. George said his time communicator for the dam in 1888. Then reported to the mayor of the city the shoddy workmanship and the poor material the contractor was using. Who was fired and a strong resilient dam was constructed.

Epilogue

About two weeks later, George and Cynthia entered the time lab at 7:30 in the morning to finally clothes the file on Ruthie. An excited Martha greeted them by saying, "It took me all night but I figured out how Ruthie's mind works. After you hired her, she went right to work and traveled back in time questioning the suspects. Ruthie wanted to get Art Boulders' side of the story. She went back in time to 1888 and began to question Art in his lab. Of course, Ruthie wore her normal skimpy attire which excited Art and the two of them wound up in bed together. Ruthie became insanely jealous when she found out that Art dated Cynthia. Rather than risk the chance of losing Art to her, Ruthie went back in time to kill Cynthia when she was walking home from church. But you George, saved Cynthia, but Ruthie tried again but failed to kill her in her sleep. George, when you married Cynthia, Ruthie decided to play interference and get you to divorce Cynthia just to make her suffer, but it didn't work. Ruthie then heard how Art was dating Miss Fits. She went into a rage and stabbed Art in the chest with the hunting knife Ruth gave him. She then tried to kill Miss Fits but we stopped her. When Ruthie tried to kill Miss. Fits the second time, that's when Ruthie wound up floating somewhere between time."

What about Don Hollister and Ruth? Where do they come in the picture?" questions, Cynthia.

"All Ruth could think about was your money Cynthia and tried to con Don into killing you so they could get it. He didn't have the heart and tried to get Ruth to do it. She made the excuse that her hands were sore and couldn't hold a knife and tried to get Art to kill Cynthia but he was more of a lover than a fighter. So, Ruth disguised herself as Cynthia and withdrew the money from the bank. Ruth couldn't have killed Art because all she was concerned about was how to get Cynthia's money. Ruthie used her feminine wiles on Rubin because she needed a place to hide her disguise. She buttered up Don to get information out of him about what Art was doing. Oh, Ruth married Don Hollister a short time later.

Cynthia question, "How could we have found Art's body in the lab before we hired Ruthie?"

"No matter where Ruthie came in during the picture the year 1890 always comes before 2020. So, when Ruthie killed Art she changed the timeline."

"That makes perfect sense stated George. Now let's go to the nearest diner and celebrate."

After George had left the time lab, swirls of energy formed in the Time Arch, Then a woman's arm slowly reached out. Followed by loud agonizing screams as Ruthie struggled desperately to free herself from her time prison.

A note from the author

The stories of Lauren and Mr. B. wasn't something that I pulled out of my imagination. It is their real testimonies of Christ in their lives.

On Aug 6, 2018, the Lord took Lauren home to be with him. The final page in Lauren's story reads: Lauren B. Brideau, 56, of Bristol, passed away peacefully Monday evening August 6, 2018. She was the beloved wife of Gary T. Brideau. Lauren was born in New Haven on November 10, 1961, the daughter of the late Lawrence and Nancy (Buckley) O'Brien. She had been a 911 dispatcher for the town of Hamden. She was a member of the Wolcott Christian Life Center. A good Christian woman, Lauren stood strong for 35 years against the diseases that attacked her body until the Lord called her home.

Mr. B. or Brideau Is still serving the Lord.

Mystery in Space

by RR Roberts

Character outlines

Sharon Flowers; queen of stage is a tall well-dressed woman with short, brown hair in her 30s goes by **Trudy** And wears a black wig and makeup as a disguise

Debbie; a pudgy woman with curly reddish-brown hair in her mid-twenty and caring a backpack full of equipment.

Sally Pennington: a medium height woman, in her late twenties with long light brown hair and loves a good cup of coffee.

A fogger; a cylinder out of her backpack six-inch-tall and an inch halt in diameter, placed a rounded cover on the top.

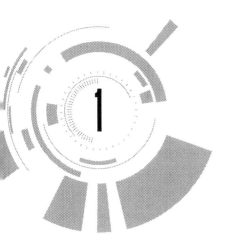

1

Fun without the Sun

Sally, a young energetic slender woman with short dark brown hair bounced out of bed early that morning thinking. yes! Today is the day I start my vacation aboard the cruise saucer ship Eternity. A whole three weeks full of fun and exciting planets to visit. Plus, exotic nights dining in the ship's Starlight Lounge.

As she packed her suitcase her videophone rang that sent a cold chill up her spine. She answered joyfully, "Oh, hi Judy, I just finished packing and was about to dart out the door."

"Girl, are you sure you want to go on the ship Eternity? I've heard some bizarre things about that ship," Her girlfriend calmly cautioned.

"What can happen? Besides, I never listen to gossip."

Concerned for her friend's safety she replied. "Those rumors aren't fairy-tales, they're true. If I were you, I'd go to the beach or something like that. But, stay as far as you can from the saucer ship Eternity."

Sally smiled and waved to her friend. Then blurted outs, "See you when I get back, bye!"

She grabbed her suitcases, and darted out the door, eager to start her vacation. On the way, in the taxicab the same cold chill rapidly made its way up her back causing the hairs on her neck to stand on end as the thoughts of impending doom flashed through her mind. And muttered, "Thanks a lot Judy for spoiling my good mood,"

As the cab came to a screeching halt in front of the spaceport terminal, she jumped out quickly, gave the cabby his fare, and rushed through the station eager to board her flight. A man holler, "Watch out!" Sally turned around with a jerk, as a cart full of luggage plowed into her. Her bags went flying over her head, as the cart sent her tumbling to the floor. She opened her eyes to see the word, 'DIE,' written in bold red print, on a black suitcase. She let out a horrendous scream fearing the worst. A young man reached down and helped her to her feet. "Are you alright ma'am?" the young man asked.

Sally nodded yes, as she; wobbly found a nearby seat to collect herself. The man then introduced himself and said, "My name is Don Isidro Everest. If there's anything I can do for you just let me know.

Sally jumped to her feet, swatted the man with her purse, and hollered, "You scared me out of twenty years growth with those initials on your baggage! Did you have to pick the color red?"

Stunned over her statement, he queried, "What do you mean by a stupid remark like that?"

"Are you dense, as well as clumsy? Think about it?" Then she stormed off muttering, "The guy should be in a horror movie with a monogram like that."

She handed the agent her ticket, then stepped on the swift-moving walkway, that, whisked her one mile down the tarmac, to the awaiting cruise saucer spaceship, Eternity. As she gazed skyward at the enormous ship, slowly filling her view. Suddenly, the feeling of being infinitesimal loomed over her like a dark cloud. As she passed under the massive hull of the Entryway, the same icy chill brought goosebumps to her flesh.

Once inside the colossal ship, the glittering red, blue, and yellow lights on the Ambrosia ice-cream table made her forget about the difficulty she had in getting there. An android porter approached her and said politely, "May I take your bags to your cabin for you ma'am?" The ship will be disembarking in a half-hour, so stay here and enjoy yourself. Just remember, your cabin is located on the first floor, number one-o-five.

With a heaping bowl of ice cream, Sally wandered to the ship's layout and read; this thing has five Olympic size swimming pools, whatever that means a tanning deck for a gorgeous tan, three snack bars, and the famous forward Starlight lounge. Sally muttered, "The first thing I'm going to do is get a tan. Then I'm gonna lie around the pool for a couple of days, sucking down cold drinks. But right now, I think I'll go to my room and relax."

On her way to her room, she bumped into a young lady with short dark brown hair about her age named Trudy, and instantly the two were friends. A short time later, Sally excused herself and went to her room, where she found a bubbling hot tub beckoning her.

Within seconds Sally had donned a one-piece bathing suit and jumped in the tub to soak away the aches and pains of the day. Within a few minutes, she drifted off to sleep.

An hour later she was suddenly awakened by the android porter glaring down at her.

She let forth a dreadful screamed at the sight of the cold expression etched on his face. He quickly reached into the hot tub and hauled her out and began to drag her out of her cabin. Halfway across the room, she screamed, "Let me go you overgrown toaster!" Then managed to squirm out of the android's grasp. She raced across the suite, grabbed the quilt off the bed, and tossed it over the robot's head, and knocked it to the floor. When she had dialed the second number on the video phone for help, the android porter came up behind her, grabbed her around the waist, and begin to drag her off.

Suddenly, the android straightened up and started to shake violently then tumbled to the deck taking Sally with him. Springing to her feet ready to defend herself. She spotted her new friend Trudy behind the android rapidly jabbing a metal shaft into the android's back.

Sally bellowed, "Way to go, girl! Thanks for saving my bacon. But you can stop now. I think it's dead."

Her friend replied, "I heard a commotion coming from your room so I came to help." She tossed Sally her bathrobe and said, "Put this on before the captain arrives, there will most likely be a lot of questions, which I hope you have answers for. Now…tell me the truth, are you one of those sick puppies that hates androids?"

Sally picked up the comforter, placed it back on the bed and plopped herself down on it and stated, "I was relaxing in the tub, the next thing I knew that piece of garbage was dragging me off, for no reason at all."

Trudy glanced down at the water all over the deck. "No doubt about that. However, androids just don't break into someone's room and go berserk. There has to be a reason."

Sally inquired, "Are you calling me a liar?"

"No! That's not what I mean. I think there's something funny going on aboard this ship and I don't mean funny ha-ha."

At that time a tall man, dressed in a pale yellow uniform casually strolled in and announced, "I'm Captain Ned, Why is one of my android lying on the floor with a steel pole rammed in his back? You had better have some good answers miss, or you'll be spending the rest of your life paying for the damages."

Sally stuck her foot in the captain's face and hollered, "See those bruises on my ankle? That overgrown toaster of yours did that when he barged into my room while I was in the hot tub and tried to drag me off. I even have the scrapes on my back where he hauled me out of the tub.

Ned grabbed the back of her robe to check the scrapes himself. Sally swiftly spun around slapped him in the face and bellowed, "Keep your hands to yourself, mister! If you want to peek, ask first!"

The captain then asked, "Do you mind if I see the marks for myself?" She smiled then answered, "Yes I do, send a female nurse in to examine me."

Ned calmly replied, "That's okay, I believe you and I'm sorry for the intrusion," then started to leave the room. Trudy rushed over to Ned seized his left arm and bellowed, "Is that all you are going to do is say you're sorry? For a captain, you have a poor attitude about things. Your first concern should be for the safety of the passengers and crew."

The captain casually replied, "I'm concerned what more do you want of me?"

Trudy snapped back, "What are you going to do about crazed android porters, running around this ship attacking people" Or do I call the press?"

Ned sighed, then said, "Okay, okay, from here on, everything is free for you to miss Sally."

She quickly replied, "What about my friend Trudy, doesn't she deserve a reward? After all, she's the one who stopped that thing." Pointing to the android on the floor.

Ned slowly reached into his pocket, handed Sally two cards, and huffed, "Anytime you want to buy something just present these cards and there will be no charge. Now if you two ladies will excuse me, I have a ship to tend to. Oh! I'll have maintenance remove the android, just don't touch anything on it."

After the captain had left, Sally quickly reconfigured the electronic lock on her cabin door by attaching a thumb plate to the lock, bypassing the override system on the door, so the door would open with her thumbprint. She then rushed over to the android porter lying on the floor and began to search him before Maintenance dragged it away.

Puzzled over what her friend was doing Trudy inquired, "Did he take something of yours?"

Sally took a white piece of paper out of his inside pocket and stated, "Nope, this is what I'm looking for, I hope." She handed it to Trudy and questioned, 'What do you make of it? It's just a bunch of numbers with a letter next to it like here it says one-o-five K"

Trudy stared at her card and muttered, "I don't know about you, but right about now in the Stardust Room is a buffet to die for and it's free. I'm about to seriously blow my diet. Coming?"

"Let's go stuff ourselves, Sally replied. Then hollered, "Wait! First things first, we need to reconfigure your lock to your thumbprint. Then we can go!"

As the two women casually walked down the hall Sally pointed to the floor, "Those long marks in the rug look like someone was dragged from their room unconscious."

"Ah....girl now, you're scaring me. You act as if somebody is going to drag us off and do despicable things to our bodies." Concerned about the marks in the rug Sally paid no attention to her friend's fearful remarks, as she bent down to examine them, "If I miss my guess those marks lead right to that room. Let's go check it out!"

2

What goes Bump in the Night.

Sally rushed to the door and knocked on it, with no results. She then gently pushed the door open, to find it empty.

Trudy commented, "I think this is my friend Debbie's room. She told me that she wasn't feeling good and was going to stay in for the night. Sally scanned the cabin as she slowly crept in, "Maybe your friend changed her mind?"

Trudy picked up a pile of clothes and replied, "Yeah right! Like she's walking around the halls in her nightclothes. I don't think so! Besides, there's something wrong here but I can't figure it out just yet."

Sally picked up a half-written letter from off the bed and said, "By the looks of things she was in the middle of writing a letter to home. But what is strange is there is a scribble line going off the page, as if she were attacked from behind and dragged off."

Sally then screamed, "Oh my gosh!" And sprinted out the door and down the hall following the drag marks in the rug. Stopping only for a moment to wait for Trudy. She then barged through a door marked Nurses Station.

Trudy whispered, "Girl, are you nuts? This is a nurse's station; you can't barge in ready to tear the place apart!"

A woman in her mid-50s with salt and pepper hair entered the room from another doorway and questioned, "Is there anything I can do for you ladies?"

Paying no attention to the nurse, Sally carefully scanned the room, looking for a body but found nothing.

Trudy placed her hand on Sally's back and said, "Let's get out of here and get something to eat before it's all gone. Debbie's most likely off sunning herself on the tanning deck."

Just then, they heard a groan coming from the next room. Sally swiftly rushed into the next room just as an Android was slicing open Debbie's abdomen.

Sally screamed, "Stop!" Trudy quickly leaped on the robot's back and gave his neck a quick twist, sending the artificial life form onto the floor in convulsions. Sally bandage the gash in Debbie's stomach than wrapped her up in the bedsheet and helped her out the door quickly glancing around the nurse's station, and shouted, "Trudy! Grabbed the healing equipment!" and rushed out.

Back in Sally's room, she replaced the hot tub cover, then gently placed Debbie on it. Taking an object shaped like an electric razor stated, "Trudy, hold the incision closed while I use the Healing Generator to close the incision?"

After several hours had passed, Debbie sat up and inquired, "What happened? The last thing I remember is being dragged off by some crazed android."

"They were about to slice you open. Do you know why?"

Trudy tossed Debbie some clothes, and asked, "Do you remember anything else?"

"All I remember is, lying on my bed writing a letter when someone grabbed me and dragged me off. I do remember someone saying something about liver and heart, but I just had a checkup, and everything was fine," replied Debbie.

Trudy picked up the bloody sheet that Debbie was wrapped in and remarked, "You're dead, and rushed out of the room with it coming back ten minutes later grinning like the cat that just ate the canary.

Sally inquired, "What's up?"

Trudy chuckled devilishly, "I placed the bloody sheet by an airlock then rubbed some blood on the airlock controls making it look like Debbie was sucked out into space."

Looking disappointed, Debbie commented, "I was hoping to see a little more of things besides a stateroom."

Sally remarked, "You could go back to your room, and wind up on the chopping block again." then inquired, "What's your stateroom number"

"One hundred. Why," replied Debbie.

Sally pulled the paper out of her pocket she took from the porter earlier and commented, "Next to your room number is, L and L, two, K, what do you suppose that could mean?"

Trudy shrugged her shoulders and muttered, "Search me, It could mean, 'Large Lady, two Kids.' All that mystery talk is making me hungry."

Debbie piped up and asked, "What about me? Do I have to stay in this dumb stateroom, for the duration of the voyage?"

Trudy bellowed as she rushed off, "I've have an idea, I'll be right back." Returning five minutes later with a dark blue, two-foot square case, and stated, "Girl, when I'm finished with you, your own mother won't even recognize you." Then opened up the case revealing an elaborate makeup kit.

Sally exclaimed, "You're a makeup artist! That's fantastic."

Trudy muttered softly, "Now let's see, which nose will look good on you, and took out one, and positioned it on Debbie's face to see how it looked.

Debbie commented loudly, "Wow! What a honker! I could double as a weathervane with that one. Could you at least give me an idea what I am going to look like when you're finished with this makeover?"

Trudy then pulled out a fake button nose and glued it on Debbie, and stated, "You, my girl, are going to be a blond bombshell, with a figure that will stop a clock."

Curious, Debbie inquired, "How do I know this will work?"

Trudy leaned back and removed her black wig showing her short brown hair, then said, "You don't think I actually go around looking this horrible now, do you? My real name is Sharon Flowers."

Debbie cried out, "Not thee Sharon Flowers, Queen of stage and screen?" She nodded yes, then declared, "Debbie, right now I need to get this makeup on you. Remember, you blow your cover, it's the morgue for you."

After finishing the disguise, Trudy left the room for a while then came back and tossed some clothes and padding at Debbie and said, "Here, put this sparkly red dress on over the padding."

Debbie waddled out of the bathroom fifteen minutes later and commented, "Am I allowed to exhale in this thing?"

Trudy fastened a small computer board to the inside of the blond wig then placed it on Debbie and said, "I put a small transceiver in your wig that will trick the security DNA scanners. Remember, you are now the fashion queen Lola."

Debbie cocked her head to one side and inquired, "They'll know I'm a fraud when they don't see my name on the passenger list."

Sally laugh quietly and bragged, "Thanks to my great computer hacking skills Lola is officially a passenger who bunks with me, now let's eat."

As the girls entered the lounge, Debbie whispered to Trudy, "What about my voice? It's a dead giveaway."

"Don't worry, they won't be paying attention to that, just speak softly and everything will be fine."

After being in the Starlight Lounge for twenty minutes, Debbie sauntered to Captain Ned's table. Sally had just finished a plate of food and was on her way up for seconds when she bumped into Don and grumbled, "You again! What, no baggage cart to run me down this time? Do everyone a favor and hunt a cemetery or something."

"Look, I'm very sorry for running you over earlier, okay. Can I make it up to you somehow?"

Forcing a Smile, Sally poked her finger in Don's chest and calmly said, "Do you like word games? I do. Let's play one with our initials, okay. Mine are S.M.E. and yours are D.I.E. Now if I add two "e" in front of the letter "s" I come up with, 'see me die.' Now buzz off loser before I call security and have you locked up for impersonating a human."

Trudy tapped Sally's shoulder, "Who's the cute guy?"

"Thrust me you don't want to know," answered Sally. She then glanced over at Debbie and uttered, "I think we need to get miss hormones back to her room before she blows it."

The ship's com system gave off several pleasant tones then a female voice said, "We will be landing on Pylee shortly and will be there for six hours. Before leaving for Avalon Prime."

Sally then caught sight of a woman in her mid-thirty, sitting three tables away from her constantly rubbing her left arm. She approached her and questioned, "Excuse me, ma'am, I'm a nurse, is there something wrong with your arm? I noticed you've been rubbing it allot."

The woman nervously replied, "I don't know what's wrong. It started this afternoon after I woke from my nap. At first, I thought my arm had just fallen asleep. But that was hours ago and it's still numb."

Sally brought the woman into the hall where there was more light and examined her arm then said, "The reason why you can't feel anything with it, is it's a state-of-the-art artificial arm."

"What are you talking about? I don't have a fake limb."

"Ma'am, by the looks of it your arm was amputated and this artificial arm was attached a short while ago. Are you sure you didn't have the operation done just before the trip and it slipped your mind because of all the excitement," Sally tenderly questioned?

Trudy tapped Sally on the shoulder and said, "Lola, ah, Debbie wants to stay with the captain. She says that she may be able to obtain some information from him. Is there anything wrong?"

Sally bid the woman goodbye, then asked, "You wanna hear something strange? That woman I was just talking to, forgot she had her arm replaced with an artificial one."

Trudy questioned, "What's so funny about that?"

"Have you ever forgotten an operation? I don't know about you but I'm going back to my room and change into something that has some room to move, then I'm going to do some investigating," replied Sally.

Later that night, Sally and her friends made their way to the Turbo lift. Where Trudy quietly inquired, "Sally, will you please tell me again why we are going up to the tanning deck at this time of night?"

"I want to look around," replied Sally.

The lift door slowly slid open to a vast dark room. Sally whispered, "Find the lights so we can see where we're going."

"Cover your eyes," commented Trudy and then flipped the switch. The deck was Instantly flooded with a warm yellow glow as the tanning lamps illuminated the deck lined with langue chairs. Sally pointed a woman lying down, halfway across the deck, and shouted, "Over there, Trudy gasped, "That Looks like Debbie!"

The two rushed across the enormous room to the blonde woman who had blood dripping from her midsection. Sally flipped her over and froze in horror as her stomach fell out of a two-foot opening In her abdomen.

Trudy swiftly turned around and immediately lost her dinner, as Sally methodically inspected the body and stated, "Her, kidneys, and liver, have been removed and no it's not Debbie."

The women looked at each other wide-eyed as they heard the turbo lift door open. Debbie then bellowed from the elevator, "Do you know how difficult you guys are to track down? By the way, what are you two doing up here anyway?" When she spotted the mutilated woman she cried, "Gross! Who is it?" Just then, they heard the turbo lift move. Sally stated loudly, "Quick on the other side of the deck is a Utility Room, we can hide in there."

Trudy commented as the three women raced across the open deck, "Debbie, I see you changed your clothes. May I ask why you decided not to play Lola?"

"I like to breathe, it's a bad habit I have," replied Debbie.

"How come you decided to keep the blond wig?"

"I like it. Is there something wrong with that?"

Sally interrupted and whispered, "Will you two shut up before you get us all killed.

3

Mangled, but Alive

Sally pushed on the door to the Utility Room and muttered, "Drats! It's locked."

Debbie bellowed, "Wait, I got it," then backed up several feet to get a good running start. Sally tried to motion to her that she had another idea, however, Debbie hollered, "Gangway!" and charged for the door, shoulder first, slamming into the solid door as hard as she could. Then whimpered, "Ouch, I think I just broke something."

Trudy questioned, "What, the door?"

Debbie grumbled, "No, my shoulder. Man, that smarts!"

Sally growled, "Will you two please, stop fooling around." She then took out the Healing Generator, turned it up to full power, and waved it in front of the lock several times, unlocking the door. As the door flew open the three rushed in searching for a place to hide.

Debbie questioned, "How did you do that?"

"I picked up a few tricks in med school, that they don't teach you in the classroom, now, shut up and hide and please, stay away from the electrical panels." warned Sally.

Debbie muttered to herself, "Duh! What does she think we are, morons? Like I'm going to stick my hand in a high voltage box, just for grins and chuckles."

Sally slid under a row of shelving, while Trudy ducked behind some heavy machinery. Debbie quickly opened a long wooden container and hopped in. After closing the lid, she felt a cold clammy hand on her face. She gasped as her eyes bugged out when she realized that she was sharing the box with a corps. She swiftly covered her mouth to smother her scream as she whimpered softly, hoping no one would hear her. After ten minutes of torture, Debbie sprang out of the box. Trudy stood up and asked, "What's wrong with you?"

Debby fretfully replied, "Eeeewwww, I just jumped in a box with a dead man!"

Trudy sarcastically replied, "Is that all?" Then glanced in the carton and stated, "Hey, you're right! He is dead."

Sally crawled out from under the shelves and slowly opened the door to see if the coast was clear. Then whispered, "The lights are out, which means he's gone."

Suddenly, a hand seized her arm and yanked her forward sending her sprawling on the floor, several feet away. As she went to stand along steel pole caught her in the midsection, knocking the wind out of her. After the lights came on, Don Isidro Everest was standing over her glaring down at her with a metal pole in his hand.

She moaned, "Why?"

He let out a sinister chuckle than answered, "Because, you're in the way. Then brought the metal pipe down across her chest. She screamed in agony as she tried to block it with her arm.

Don laughed devilishly, "Bye, bye, my darling." Then he raised the pipe to crush her skull.

Debbie charged out of the Utility Room and crashed into Don with her shoulder, sending him tumbling to the floor. She then leaped on top of him, to try to wrestle the pipe away from him. However, as she was in midair he caught her in the stomach with his knee, then hurled her over his head sending her crashing into several lounge chairs. Just as he stood up, Trudy smashed a chair over his back. He slowly turned around, smiled at her, and rammed the end of the pipe in her stomach. Then watched with glee as she slowly crumpled to the floor. By now, Sally had propped herself up against the wall cradling her injured arm. Don casually walked to her saying, "Time to die my darling." Then raised the pipe high over his head for the final blow.

Sally quickly pulled out a long metal fingernail file from her sleeve and rammed it in his throat. Don staggered backward, desperately gasping for air. Determined to finish her off, he held his hand over his throat, and with the other, he tried to swing the pipe.

Trudy quickly grabbed the pipe and yanked it out of his hand. Landing a devastating blow to his chest, which sent him tumbling to the floor.

Sally staggered several feet to a chair, and slowly sat down sobbing. Her two friends hobbled over to her and inquired, "Can you make it to the nurse's station?"

Sally sobbingly just nodded her head, yes. Then cried, "I'm a nurse. I'm supposed to save likes! Why did we have to kill him? Why? There had to be another way, besides taking a human life!"

Debbie removed her bandanna and placed it on Sally's gash in her head, then she said tenderly, "He would have killed us, we had to defend ourselves."

Sally sighed, then replied, "It seems so strange, after working so hard for so long. I turned around and kill someone."

Trudy grimaced as she took a deep breath then said, "Look at it this way, you most likely saved hundreds of people's lives on this ship."

Sally gave out a groan as she stood up and hobbled towards the turbo lift.

Debbie tapped her lightly on the arm and said, "Wait a minute, I got an idea.' Then rushed off. Coming back later carrying a man's shirt.

Sally questioned as Debbie made a sling for her arm, "Where did you get that from?"

Debbie chuckled slightly, then replied, "From the dead guy in the box."

Trudy glared at her but remained silent.

Debbie commented, "What? We need it more than he does, besides, I'll bet he'll never know it's gone."

Trudy chuckled, "You're a sick puppy, you know that?"

The three hobbled their way back to Sally's room where she made a video phone call to Judy on Avalon Prime.

Judy cried out in horror, "Good Lord!" when she saw Sally's mangled figure come into view. After the shock had worn off Judy cried out, "What happened to you that must have been some party?"

Sally moaned as she took a breath, then said, "Judy, this is a matter of life or death! Please! Call the police, and have them waiting for the cruise ship, Eternity, on Avalon Prime when it lands. There's a mad killer aboard slaughtering people for their body parts." Without warning, the video screen went black.

Debbie questioned, "What proof, do we have that they are harvesting human organs for money?"

Sally pulled out the paper she took from the android porter and said, "Next to stateroom one hundred, there is L and L, two, K."

Debbie rapidly answered, "We've been through all this. What are you getting at?"

"Where it says, L and L, two K, means lung and liver, two kidneys. Next to my room, number one-o-five, there is H, K, L. Which means, they wanted my heart, kidneys, and lungs, right now, I like to keep using them. We have to put a stop to this before we reach Avalon Prime." She slowly scanned her room looking for an escape just as the security guards began to pound on her door. Sally then whispered quickly, the hot tub. We get in and cover it over."

Debbie inquired, "What about the water? Won't it spill out with all of us in it?"

Sally slid the cover off and said, "I drained it this morning, after I used it, now hush, before they know we're in here."

Sally maneuvered the cover back in place concealing them in the tub as guards exploded into the room brandishing high-powered energy rifles. The leader bellowed, "Search the room, they've got to be here somewhere!"

Packed in the tub like sardines, the three women silently and tearfully pleaded, "Lord, please don't let them find us in here."

After things had settled down, Debbie gradually lifted the lid, to see if the coast was clear. Then sprang out and exclaimed, "Fresh air, no offense, but boy, do you guys wreak!"

Trudy snapped back, "You don't smell like a bed of roses yourself!"

Debbie stuck her nose in the air and stated, "I don't stink, I'm just slightly odiferous."

"Ah. What's the difference," replied Trudy.

Sally interrupted and said, "It just sounds better that's all." She then sobbed as she gradually scanned her stateroom growling, "They destroyed my room!" Then picked her light blue evening gown up off the floor, with a black footprint on it and roared, "Will you look at what they did to my new evening dress! It's ruined!"

At that moment, the captain of the guards stepped in the shattered doorway and fired a shot just missing Trudy's head. He then brushed the stuff off the bed, and relaxed on it and said, "My men should be back soon, but, for now, you three can stand over there against the wall."

With sad puppy dog eyes, Sally sobbed, "Do you mind if I sit down? I think I broke my arm and busted some ribs." The guard exclaimed, "Oh! Maybe I can be of some assistance." He slowly strolled to her smiling and thinking sadistically, One blast with my gun and I won't have to worry about her." When he was several feet from her, she kicked him as hard as she could, where it would hurt the most. The guard groaned as he toppled to the floor, clutching himself. Trudy ripped the gun out of his hand, then belted him in the head, knocking him out. She grasped the rifle by the barrel and rushed over to the door, ready for whomever.

As the first guard came charging through the door, Trudy hollered, "Batter up," and hit his mid-section, sending him tumbling to the floor. Debbie quickly caught the gun, as it flew out of his hand and began shooting the other guards as they stormed the room.

Grimacing because of her busted ribs. Sally slowly reached down, picked up one of the guard's sidearm, and hollered, "Now, it's payback time. They are going to pay, for ruining my vacation."

4

Sweet Revenge

Now armed, the trio hobbled their way out of the demolished room and down the hallway. Sally gave out a mournful, moan as they cautiously entered the medic station. Suddenly, a woman doctor rushed into the dispensary and abruptly stopped. Her jaw dropped to the floor as an expression of horror froze on her face and said, "I've heard of people partying hard, but don't you think you women overdid it slightly?"

Debbie replied sarcastically, "Just a tad. Do you really think we'd get this wasted while partying? Not on your life."

The doctor queried, "Then pray tell, what in the world happened to you three?"

Sally interrupted, "Do you know someone by the name of Don?"

"That sadistic monster. If I could, I'd shove him out the nearest airlock, for what he and the captain are doing to the passengers aboard this cruise ship."

Sally curiously questioned, "Oh, the captain is in on it, too?"

"By the way, my name is Kate. Could you please hand me the skin regenerator next to your right hand. I can start treating your injuries."

Kate was taking care of Trudy's gash when she warned, "You guys need to be very careful of Don. I overheard the captain tell him to get rid of three troublesome women. Which I believe are you three."

Debbie quickly replied, "Thanks for the tip-off. But you're a bit late.

We already met up with Don and made sure he will never hurt anyone ever again."

Sally let go of a shriek as tears filled her eyes, as Kate lightly pushed on her ribcage to check for injuries.

Kate, inquired, "Did that hurt?"

Sally harshly replied, "Duh! What kind of a stupid question was that? Of course, it did. Now fix me up, so I can get back to enjoying what's left of my vacation!"

After fixing Sally's busted ribs and arm with a bone regenerator, Kate questioned, "What about the brains behind the operation? Are you just going to let him go free?"

Debbie piped up and asked, "We thought it was Don and the androids porters who were killing and disfiguring the passengers."

Kate affirmed, "Trust me on this, Ned is a sick puppy that needs to be stopped and soon."

Debbie calmly questioned, "How do you know all this?"

"I can't tell you," Kate hurriedly answered,

"You can't, or you won't tell us!" stated Trudy.

Kate sobbed, "I can't tell you because if I do he'll kill my daughter."

Sally slowly picked up her proton pistol, pointed it at Kate, and stated, "If you don't tell us what you know about the people being mutilated aboard this ship. We'll make sure to include you when the police raid the ship once we land on Avalon Prime."

Reluctantly, Kate stated, "Captain Ned is a heavy gambler and is in hock up to his eyeballs with the mob. He created a situations causing accidents aboard ship to injure people. Then he told me to give them a sedative to put them to sleep so he could remove their organs for profit. I told him that I would not have anything to do with his sadistic scam. That's when he kidnapped my daughter and threatened to kill her if I didn't go along with him."

Kate then handed Sally a small oblong computer storage crystal and said, "Everything you need to convict Ned is on this crystal."

Trudy bellowed, "No hard feelings, then belted her with the butt of her rifle. Sending Kate sprawling on the floor out cold.

Shocked over Trudy's action, Sally questioned, "What did you do that for?"

"To protect her," replied Trudy.

"Ah, weren't we supposed to hide her? Instead of clobbering her like a common criminal," Inquired Sally.

Trudy casually replied, "True, however, if it looks like we forced a confession out of her, he'll think twice about killing her and the daughter."

"That's an unorthodox way of doing it but it just may work," stated Sally.

"Now on to the next subject, capturing Ned. Any ideas?" questioned Sally as she checked her rifle to make sure the power pack was fully charged.

"We could use the ship's security system in Security Control to locate Kate's daughter." Suggested Debbie, "With all the cameras we're sure to spot her"

"How do we get there without being spotted," questioned Trudy.

Sally upholstered her pistol and bellowed, "We blast our way through, that's how. If you don't like it, you can go back to your room and sulk for all I care. It makes me furious every time I think about the money I spent on this trip. I paid for three weeks of fun and excitement. Instead, I've been dragged around by half-crazed robots, shot at by some nut, and had my ribs busted. Because some maniac wants to sell some body parts. This is what I think." She then muttered softly, "Safety off," power to maximum." Then gave out with a loud scream. A brilliant beam of white energy shot out of the gun, down the hallway, and smashed into a painting, vaporizing it. Simultaneously the other two girls stated, "We're right behind you."

Trudy whispered, "Yeah! Way behind you!" Then stepped back three feet just in case Sally attempted to do something radical. Like attack, three armed android porters single-handedly.

Upon reaching the security room Trudy inquire, "What now? Do we burst through the door guns blazing?" Debbie politely knocked on the door and said coyly, "Excuse me, is anybody in there? I have a slight problem and I was wondering if you could help me."

The door slowly opened revealing a dark room filled with flat-screen monitors, showing every part of the ship. Trudy commented, "Or we could just knock, and pray they don't blow us away."

Sally practically shoved her rifle barrel up the security guard's nose as he answered the door, while the other two girls rushed in and stunned the other guards. With the guards now out of the way. They set themselves to search for Kate's little girl. As the three intensely studied every detail on each monitor screen, in hopes to discover a clue. All they could see were empty hallways and a vacant Starlight Lounge.

Debbie inquired, "I wonder where everybody went to?"

Sally picked a note up from off the desk that read, "Urgent situation, quietly, get all the passengers in life pods we have to evacuate the ship, because of three crazed women killers."

Debbie commented, "You mean we have to be on the lookout for three crazy women? How did they get on board?"

Trudy nudged her in the shoulder saying, "Hey numb-numb! They're talking about us."

"Oh, however, with everyone gone, it should make our job a lot easier."

Sally sharply replied, "Don't be too sure of that."

Suddenly, someone pounded on the door and hollered, "Come out peacefully and give yourselves up."

Sally shouted back, "Why? So, you can carve us up like a Christmas ham? I don't think so."

, "When I say so, open the door and be ready to shoot." Sally whispered to Trudy, "Better yet, shoot right through the door on the count of three."

The darkroom suddenly lit up as three protons guns blasted the door to the security room. In mere seconds, the door shattered into millions of pieces throwing the guards back against the wall.

Sally took the lead as she stepped over the men scattered on the hall floor, and said, "I know where the girl is being held! Just remember one thing. If it moves shoot first and asked questions later."

At the captain's quarters, Sally blasted the lock then kicked the door open rescuing the young girl. Debbie inquired as they left with the doctor's daughter, "Did they really abandon ship?"

Trudy added, "I haven't seen any passengers, and this place is too quiet if you ask me."

Sally holstered her weapon, leaned up against the wall to think for a while. Then roared, "We need to get to the bridge and fast!"

The three women stood motionless for ten seconds as the turbo lift door slid open to the bridge devoid of personnel. Sally recovered from the shock ordered, "Debbie, Take the scanning station. Trudy! Take the pilot's seat! Maybe between the three of us, we may be able to land this bucket of bolts."

Debbie questioned, "Sally, ah, where do you want me to take the scanner?"

Sally gave a loud sigh then said, "Don't be a moron! Just operate the stupid thing!"

Sally fiddled around with the buttons on the arm of the captain's chair for a while to try and contact help. Suddenly the admiral of the Space Patrol flashed on the forward screen and asked, "Can I help you?"

Sally tried to keep her composure as she replied, "I sure hope so. I need to know how to land this jalopy. It seems that the captain and everyone has fled the ship, leaving us aboard to die."

The admiral queried, "Do you have any experience flying?"

An agitated Sally replied, "If I didn't need help flying this thing, I wouldn't be asking for you. Now would I?"

The admiral calmly questioned, "What's your course, and speed?"

"My course is right where you are! The ship's speed is as fast as it can go! How am I to know what's going on with this thing. I never even stepped foot in a spaceship let alone fly one! Now help me land this bucket of bolts before this thing turns your beautiful spaceport into a smoking pile of rubble."

Trudy interrupted, "I think we are traveling just over the speed of light."

"You have got to slow the ship down," replied the admiral, "Can you find the reverse thrusters controls?"

Trudy nervously scanned the console in front of her. Then tapped the section marked thrusters. Catapulting the ship forward to twice the speed of light. Then muttered, "Ah, Sorry."

Sally sighed, then said, "Admiral, The controls are like Greek to us. Without knowing what's what, you might want to evacuate the spaceport because we are coming in hot!"

At that moment, Kate entered the bridge with her daughter and questioned, "Who's piloting the ship?"

Sally mournfully replied, "No one. We have the admiral on the view screen but we can't follow his instructions because we don't know what we're doing."

Kate jumped in the pilot's chair and stated, "I took a few lessons in piloting maybe I can help. Then tapped in a command slowing the ship down to one hundred and eighty-six thousand miles a second. Looking more concerned, the admiral reported, "You have got to slow down the ship even more in order to land safely."

Kate replied, "Admiral! I've slowed the ship down and we're ready to enter the flight path for landing. What do I do next?"

"Next, you need to lower the landing struts, and descend vertically."

After trying frantically for three minutes to engage the landing struts, she stated, "Sorry no can do sir. The landing struts are offline. Prepare for a crash landing because we are coming in fast, hot, and out of control."

Fire engulfed, the Pleasure ship Eternity as it streaked through Avalon Prime's atmosphere out of control. At the last moment Kate hollered, "Computer, engage manual controls!"

A joystick moved up between Trudy's legs. Kat then commanded, Trudy, slowly pull back on the stick until the ship is at thirty degrees."

The ship plowed through a dense forest. Then skipped along the ground coming to rest three feet in front of the spaceport's control tower.

Wobbly, the women left the wrecked spaceship and walked up to the admiral who greeted Kate and her daughter with open arms.

However, he glared at Sally and her friends and commanded, "Arrest them for the murder of Don, and the countless other poor unsuspecting passengers they cut up."

In raged Sally screamed, "Now wait just a cotton-picken minute! I have proof that Captain Ned is a sick sadistic psychopath who's been going around murdering people. Stealing their organs to pay off his huge gambling debt. The ship's doctor Kate, will testify to that in a court of law. The admiral thought for a moment then stated, "Most likely you obtained her confession under duress."

At that moment Captain Ned emerged from the crowd grinning and bragged, "I've been a spaceship captain for fifteen years and all that time I have never seen anyone as depraved as those three women."

As the Police were dragging the women away, a tall man with brown curly hair stepped out of the crowd, with another stout man with red hair.

bellowed, "Just a moment! You have the wrong ones. Let them go! I'm The Galaxy Sentinel, and this is my partner Sam. Ned, you don't exist anymore. Your life as you know has just come to an end. It's time for the judgment."

Sam interrupted, "Admiral Delay. Are you still conning the people? Thor do we have room for one more slimeball."

"Sure do, Sam, call for retrieval. Oh, Sally, I'll take the evidence Kate gave you on Ned." In a blinding flash of pale blue light, the four vanished.

Epilogue

A man that was 6 foot six with chiseled features and broad shoulders dressed in white pants and a dark blue polo shirt. Approached the women and stated, "I presume you three are the Mystery Three Investigation Team. I'm the CEO of the company that operates the cruise ship Eternity. I'll pay each of you ladies $6000 if you will guard The saucer ship for me for two weeks. Because it will take that long to figure out how to move that pile of scrap metal."

Sally inquired, "Will the ship have power? Can we live on the ship while we're guarding it?"

"Yes, you can choose any stateroom you please and the ship will have full power. The galley will also be in full operation. Just don't allow anyone on the ship."

The women high fived each other and Sally stated, "You can't get any better than being paid for a vacation. I know one thing, I'm taking the president's suite and pig out for the next two weeks.

Trudy stated, "We need to choose who is going to take which watch."

Sally stated, "Stand watch nothing, We Lock the hatch and relax for next two weeks."

"That'll work stated." Trudy smiling.

Printed in the United States
By Bookmasters